Thirteenth Apostle

THIRTEENTH APOSTLE

Richard A. Johns

BROADMAN PRESS
Nashville, Tennessee

© 1966 • BROADMAN PRESS
Nashville, Tennessee
All rights Reserved

Second Printing

423-051

Dewey Decimal Classification: F(Fiction)
Library of Congress Catalog Card Number: 66-19908
Printed in the United States of America
3.5O6613

for

Joan

and for

Robert Hill

You must rededicate yourself to the ideals for which your father entrusted you to my keeping," said the revered Gamaliel as I stood at a window in his chambers, looking across the vast, squat reaches of Jerusalem. "You are young and a man of great potential to the service of God."

There was a light and stimulating breeze. I inhaled deeply of it and turned to face the learned man.

"I have no more the fire that once burned within me," I said. "I am like a dead man."

He leaned forward. "What of the Saul who once bested me in a class debate on the prophetic implications of Melchizedek?"

I hesitated. There was the bare trace of a smile behind the long, gray beard and something more of warmth and humor in the twinkling black eyes.

"I wasn't aware that I had won," I said.

He leaned back again. "And that was because I did not admit that you had won. How could I when I faced a class full of young men already on your side?"

I could not suppress a smile. "I thought Ephraim bar Joshua was the only one on my side," I said.

"Nonsense. They were all on your side, just as you were on the

7

side of each of them when they arose to debate the great Gamaliel."
At that he broke into a laugh, and I could not refrain from laughing
myself. It was the first time I had laughed in months. It seemed
labored and strange.

"Cheer up, my boy," he said. "Great things await the man who
can laugh in his adversity."

"And greater things the man who can best Gamaliel in a classroom
dispute," I said.

He bowed and motioned to the chair beside him. "Come and sit
down," he said.

I did as he bade me, as I always had. When I was seated he
put his fingertips to his mouth and stared through the window at the
stretch of clear blue sky which dropped behind the hill called the
Mount of Olives. The summit was barely visible above the sill. Momentarily, he turned to me, every trace of levity gone from his aged
countenance.

"What do you know of this Jesus of Nazareth?"

I hesitated.

"You have heard of Jesus of Nazareth?"

"There have been tales. Reuben bar Nahum of Joppa spoke of
him . . . a carpenter's son, blaspheming the name of God and incit-
ing heresy among the people."

"Essentially the case," nodded Gamaliel, "only his successes have,
I fear, been more widespread and have reached further into the
imaginations of the people than we, or perhaps I, had thought."

The teacher arose, walked to the center of the room beside a table
piled high with scrolls and turned.

"I saw this Jesus of Nazareth, on several occasions," he said. "I
can assure you he was no ordinary insurrectionist."

"Yes?"

Gamaliel looked slightly down, his brow furrowed as one in deep
concern. He spoke solemnly, methodically, as one almost entranced
by the words he uttered.

"I saw him once . . . make a whip of reeds and single-handedly
drive the money changers from the Temple. I heard him speak, and
though his words were revolutionary there was about them, and him,

8

a positive magnetism, an authoritative magnetism. I could not take my eyes off him while he spoke, or even afterward."

"Reuben said he claimed miraculous power."

"That is so. It is said that he opened the eyes of the blind and made the lame to walk."

I looked closely at my mentor. "With all due respect, Rabbi, it seems that you do not dismiss the folly for what it is."

"Folly . . ." He started to say more, but his voice trailed off into nothingness.

"He was crucified, was he not?" I asked.

"Yes . . . Yes, and some say rose again."

"Surely, sir . . ."

"It is what is said."

"Said by whom?"

"By his followers. Scores reported seeing him again."

I laughed. "He cast a wide spell, this one."

Gamaliel did not reply.

"What of his followers?" I asked.

"Rabble, the dregs of the earth . . . . They meet. The Jews who follow him do not forsake the ways of the law. They attend the synagogues, but they meet in secret with the Gentiles and observe certain rites."

"To what end?"

"I do not know."

"It will all die."

"I do not know . . ."

"It will die."

Gamaliel was looking at the floor and slowly moving his head side to side. "There is something about it I do not like," he said, his voice barely audible.

"Why don't you stamp it out?" I said.

He did not reply, but looked up at me as though shocked by such an outburst from one who had always displayed moderation in his presence.

"I would stamp it out, kill it in its cradle," I said.

"I am not certain that would be possible in this case," he said.

"You have not seen this thing as I have. I have advised restraint at this point."

"I would kill it, now, before it takes hold."

Gamaliel walked slowly to the window and looked out. The air blew his hair gently. He thought for a long moment, then turned. "There is a man named Stephen," he said, "a potter, who is a leader in this movement and who goes about from synagogue to synagogue preaching that this dead carpenter was the Messiah."

"Does no one withstand him—make a fool of him before the people?"

Gamaliel again did not reply. He looked at me as though he desired to speak, but then turned his head back toward the window.

"He will be this week at the synagogue of your Cilicians," he said.

"I will be there."

"He is . . . eloquent . . ."

"He cannot withstand the truth."

Rabban Gamaliel did not reply, nor did his gaze leave the stretch of the city now golden where the long shadows could not reach.

During the more than ten years of my troubled existence in Tarsus after the death of my parents, I had returned to Jerusalem only at intervals and had remained there only briefly. But on each such occasion I had made a point of stopping by the home of a man who had shown me much kindness during my student days at the college of rabbis. This was Joshua bar Zebulun, a tanner whose son Ephraim had been my closest friend. Joshua lived not far from the great palace, known still as Herod's Palace, but occupied at intervals by the procurator, Pilate.

It was my intention to ask lodging of Joshua until I could find a permanent place to reside, for Jerusalem was to be my haven until such time as God might direct otherwise. I was in nowise possessed of inner peace, though for the first time since my tragedy there seemed to be, in the strange particulars disclosed to me by Gamaliel, a glimmer of promise for a cause in which to project myself.

I hastened from the chamber of my old teacher and walked south and west for some distance, savoring the brighter prospects and enjoying the bracing atmosphere. I made my way at a quickened pace down the narrow, winding streets, past the shops of the barbers and the confectioners and delayed for a moment opposite the massive structure now inhabited by the Roman procurator.

Pontius Pilate divided his Jerusalem residence between the Palace and the Fortress Antonia, located at the northwestern corner of the Temple area. It was the time of the changing of the guard, and the reflected rays of the late evening sun danced off the polished metal of the uniforms as two guards were smartly assigned to each post.

I assumed this doubling to have been prompted by the general state of unrest surrounding the recent execution of the blaspheming Galilean and turned over again the concerned words of Gamaliel. Perhaps, I thought, this cult portended more of significance than I had allowed myself to contemplate. The wise old teacher was not given to rash assessments, and for me to have made such an assumption was impertinence quite inexcusable. There had been a time when I would not have been guilty of such a breach of good manners. On the morrow I would go to him and ask his forgiveness and perhaps seek his counsel on the proper course in dealing with this unsavory turn of events.

And yet, I could not believe it wrong to meet extremism with extremism where the things of Almighty God were concerned. Had we not as a people been singled out and invested with a holy trust embodied in the law? And must we not, then, kill at once any threat to that trust? My mind turned these things over as I surveyed the massive structure whose whimsical occupant the Roman spears were pledged to protect. I was not, of course, at that time fully aware of the part this Pontius Pilate had played in the tide of events into which I was soon to be so forcefully swept.

It was dusk when I arrived at the house of Joshua bar Zebulun. The shadows had completely shrouded the street and left only the highest tips of the buildings brushed with deep orange. I raised my hand to knock but hesitated, suddenly apprehensive. The street was quiet and deserted and I had passed only a handful of people in the last several blocks. I was not afraid, but the unusual stillness puzzled me. This had always been a busy street.

No sound now issued from within the house of Joshua. I started to steal away and perhaps seek lodging at an inn near the center of the city. I turned, then scolded myself for the absurdity and went back and rapped on the door.

There were footsteps, then the door was barely cracked and not flung open eagerly as it had always been before. Old eyes squinted from the dimly lighted interior.

"Yes," the old man said.

"Joshua?"

"Yes. Who are you?"

"Joshua, do you not know me?"

"The light is bad. Is it . . . ?"

"Saul."

"Saul of Tarsus?"

"Yes."

At that he smiled and opened to me. "Saul, my boy, come in, come in. What a wonderful surprise." He put his arms about me as he always did, and when he drew me close I saw over his shoulder that he was not alone. Seated at the end of the table at the far wall, his face half-illuminated by a lamp which sat before him, was a large, black-bearded man regarding me closely. The two had been eating.

"It is good to see you, Joshua," I said.

Joshua stepped back and examined me from head to toe. "Saul, you are thinner."

"The consequences of bachelorhood," I smiled.

"But it is good to have you here again. Come, there is someone you must meet." He shepherded me to the table, and as we approached the stranger arose. He was even larger than I had thought. "Saul, my guest Barnabas of the island of Cyprus. Barnabas, my very dear friend the rabbi Saul of Tarsus."

We bowed, and the big man said "I have heard much of Saul of Tarsus."

"From Ephraim," interjected Joshua.

"Ah, of course," I said. Ephraim had been for two years rabbi of a synagogue of Cyprus.

"Here . . . you must join us," said the old man, making place for me at the table. "There is more than enough fish and wine."

"I am intruding," I said.

"No, no."

13

"Please join us," said the man Barnabas, seating himself again.

When I looked closer I saw that the stranger was a very handsome man of forceful countenance and almost regal bearing. His robe was woven of the finest thread, but a close inspection revealed that it was frayed about the neck.

"Thank you," I said, and took the proffered chair at tableside between the two.

"It is not the time of the feast of the Passover," said Joshua, pouring wine into my glass, "so to what do we owe this pleasure?"

"I have returned to Jerusalem, Joshua, to live."

A look of perplexity came upon the wrinkled face, but gave way to a smile. "That is wonderful news," he said and he set the bottle down and seated himself.

"You arrived today?" inquired Barnabas.

"Yes, I have been with Rabban Gamaliel, then came here."

"You hear that, Barnabas?" smiled Joshua. "This young man whom I have raised from a pup, comes to Jerusalem and sees his teacher before he sees his family."

"It is . . . shameful," I said.

Joshua laughed and put his hand upon mine. "You know I was jesting, my boy," he said. "It is like old times having you here at this table."

I laughed, too, and ate heartily, for I had not tasted food since early morning. "But tell me, Joshua," I said, "what of Ephraim?"

"He is well," replied the old man. "But Barnabas can tell you more of him than I."

"Ephraim is well, as Joshua has said," Barnabas submitted, finishing the last of his wine. "You might, in fact, say that he is in every respect as one born again."

"Born again?" I looked at the big man and then at Joshua, but the old man's eyes were on his food.

"He spreads the gospel of Jesus Christ," Barnabas said.

I sat speechless.

"Saul, perhaps I can get you more fish," interrupted Joshua.

"No . . . No, thank you," I said, not really hearing my words. I could not have been more stunned if the man had said that

Ephraim had journeyed to Tarsus to participate in a Baal-worshiping orgy. I glanced quickly at Joshua, but he did not raise his head. We ate for a while in silence, and then Joshua spoke.

"But where are your belongings, my son?" he inquired of me. "You will certainly stay here with me."

I could not reply.

"Of course you will. There is ample room since Ephraim is gone, and I am alone."

I looked up at Barnabas.

"I have lodging elsewhere," he said. "I am here as a messenger, and my good friend importuned me to remain for this excellent fish and wine. And now," he said, arising, "you really must excuse me. I shall be late for the prayer service. Rabbi," he bowed, as he made to leave. "Joshua."

I bowed slightly, but did not arise. Joshua got up and escorted the man to the door. They had whispered words outside, and then Joshua reentered the room, carrying the small bag of my belongings which I had left outside.

"I found this outside the door," he said. "I am taking it to the upper room when we have finished eating. You will stay here with me, and that is the end of it."

I did not reply, but took the last of my wine and leaned back in my chair.

When the meal was finished and preparation of my room had been completed, the two of us retired to the roof to enjoy the coolness and the spectacular view of Jerusalem afforded therefrom. Joshua's house was situated in an area populated by those of some means, shopkeepers and small businessmen. He lived on a hill overlooking the Valley of Hinnom, and so choice was the situation that I counted no greater pleasure in the city than standing on that roof and surveying the myriad of lights across the broad sweep of Jerusalem. On a moonless night they were like stars reflected in a crystal lake. When there was a strong eastern breeze, as there was that night, the gentle, fragrant scent of the narcissus came at intervals from the Mount of Olives and increased the pleasure.

Joshua and I sat for some time in silence until I could no longer suppress the thing which I knew to be as much on his mind as on my own.

"Am I to understand," I said, "that Ephraim has become involved with this cult of the Galilean?"

Joshua looked down, inhaled deeply, then looked up at me and began slowly. "You have been away, Saul, while many wondrous and inexplicable things have occurred in this land."

"It would seem that I have been away too long, when a blaspheming fraud can pervert the elect of God. Ephraim, of all people! It is fantastic!"

Joshua said nothing.

"Ephraim has turned his back on God!"

"No, Saul, no. You cannot know, because you have not seen, nor heard, as—"

"As you, Joshua?"

"Yes, yes! Saul, my son, I have seen this Jesus of Nazareth feed four thousand people with seven loaves and a few small fishes . . ."

"Oh come, Joshua."

"I have, Saul. I have seen, and I ate. I was among the crowd."

"A magician's trick."

"No. I assure you, no. He worked wonders. There were other things. He made blind men see, and when he spoke . . . you felt it, inside. Never man did the things he did, or spoke as he spoke."

I shook my head. "Then he tricked you, too."

"I know what my eyes have seen and my ears have heard."

I said no more of the matter, fearing that if I did my anger might get the best of me. Never had I been more profoundly shocked. Even the death of my parents had not landed so heavily upon me, for this was worse than death. I retired that night resolved to seek out other lodging at the earliest possible moment on the following day.

Sabbath of that week found me some distance from the house of Joshua. I left before he arose the morning after our words on the roof. There was no longer any attachment between us. He had chosen a course of treason, and whatever happened to him or to his son thereafter was of no concern to me. I cast all thought of them from my mind.

There had been within me in the intervening days a raging debate as to whether my own course should be to report them to the Sanhedrin so that they might be watched, or merely to forget that I ever had known them. The latter had prevailed.

The one misgiving I had concerned Barnabas. He was such a man as could be dangerous. There had been a cold dedication in his eyes, the kind one sees in those of an extremist. I would bide my time, but at the first indication of trouble from the fanatics I would make a full report to the Temple authority.

This Sabbath I left my room in a small inn near the center of the city and walked east to the synagogue of the Cilicians which was also called the synagogue of the Libertines. This was a beautiful synagogue situated on a slight rise in the plateau near the valley of the Kidron. I had attended here frequently. It was the place of worship of my own people.

But on this day I was not cognizant of beauty nor of ought save the blasphemous outpourings of a man called Stephen. He was a fellow no taller than myself, clean shaven and by all physical accounts innocuous. But the words he said to the assembled Jews were enough to boil the blood in my veins. He spoke with unrestrained enthusiasm of justification before God by faith in this Galilean carpenter's son. As if this were not blasphemy enough, he uttered abominations concerning the destruction of the Temple. He brushed aside the law as if it were no more than a collection of guide lines and substituted that which he called "grace," or unmerited favor. Justification before God, he said, was attained not through the Law of Moses, but through faith in this Jesus of Nazareth. It was all a gift which could not be earned no matter with what fervor it was pursued. I feared lest at any moment God should send a thunderbolt through the roof, and we should all be killed for entertaining such blasphemy.

"I ask you, sirs," this Stephen continued, "to consider the words of our father David (for Stephen was a Jew): 'My God, my God, why have you forsaken me.' Were not some of you there when these very words issued from the lips of Jesus on the cross? And further, from the same psalm: 'I am poured out like water, and all my bones are out of joint: my heart is like wax; it is melted in the midst of my bowels. My strength is dried up like a potsherd; and my tongue cleaves to my jaws; and you have brought me into the dust of death.' Sirs, I submit that no more vivid description of death by crucifixion could be found, and I also submit that David, King of Israel, spoke prophetically of Jesus of Nazareth as Messiah."

"Blasphemy!" roared a voice behind me, and I jumped at the ear-splitting cry. "Blasphemy!" echoed the charge, and several arose, shaking their fists at Stephen, who did not flinch nor seem in the least shaken.

"Hear me out if you do not fear the truth!" He continued: "How many here saw the soldiers of Rome and what they did with the robe of Jesus? How many? You, Malachi," he pointed to a man on the front row, "I have heard it from your lips. They tore the robe from his body, the seamless robe, and threw dice for it. Did they not, Malachi? Tell these learned men. Yes, they threw dice for the robe of Jesus. And let me quote further from the psalm of David: 'They part my garments among them, and cast lots upon my vesture.' "

The man Stephen looked across the murmuring crowd. " ' . . . and cast lots upon my vesture'. Learned sirs, this was written centuries before the event so fresh in the minds of us all. I tell you that the Messiah was here, among us, and was rejected of his own and suffered death on the cross for the remission of sin. Accept him now. There is no sanctification by any other means."

"Stone him!" cried a man across the room. "Yes, stone him! Stone him!" roared the assembly. Two or three rose and rushed forward and laid hands on this Stephen and began pulling at him.

I arose and shouted. "No! Do not desecrate the Sabbath or this holy place of God! Stand away from the blasphemer!"

Burning eyes turned toward me. "He must be stoned!" shouted one of those who had set upon Stephen. "It is the law!"

"It is the law that he be brought before the Sanhedrin and tried," I said. "We must not sink to the level of this blasphemer by ignoring the law as he does. Let him be tried, and if he is found guilty, the law will have triumphed over blasphemy, will it not? We will see if his 'Messiah' can save him then."

"He is right," said the man next to me. "Let this blasphemer be tried fairly by the very law he condemns."

The tumult eased, and those who had leaped upon Stephen lowered their arms and stood looking toward me, as did he whom they had set upon.

"I should like to speak to this man," I said, my voice calmer. I waited as, one by one, they regained their composure and reseated themselves. When the murmuring gave way to silence I looked directly into the eyes of Stephen. My gaze did not waver as I spoke.

"Now you quote freely from our father David," I said. "So it becomes my turn . . . 'Blessed is the man who walks not in the counsel of the ungodly, nor stands in the way of sinners, nor sits in the seat of the scornful. But his delight is in the Law of the Lord: and in his Law does he meditate day and night.' "

19

"Amen," said the man seated next to me, and the word was repeated across the room.

" 'The Lord,' " I continued, " 'shall judge the people: judge me, O Lord, according to my *righteousness,* and according to my *integrity* that is within me.' "

"Amen, amen."

" 'The law of the Lord is perfect, converting the soul; the testimony of the Lord is sure, making wise the simple.' "

The words came to me and issued forth like running waters. I was as one inspired, as one with a renewed spirit of purpose.

" 'Praise you the Lord. Blessed is the man who fears the Lord, who delights greatly in his *commandments.' "

And so it went. Those things Gamaliel had entrusted to my memory while I was his student came forth as through an opened floodgate. I called upon the resources of my mind for all that I knew from David regarding sanctification by the law. And I could feel, as sentence followed sentence, the greater backing of the assembly. When my case was completed to my satisfaction, I took my seat convinced that whatever the blasphemer might say would surely be weak, and perhaps even laughable, in the face of the word of almighty God.

But Stephen showed no sign of weakness, nor of intimidation. His countenance remained as calm and as strong as it had since the moment he had begun speaking some two hours previously. "My brother," he said, "I do not come to dishonor the law of Moses and of our fathers. Indeed, the One whose name I magnify kept every jot and tittle of the law. In him there was no sin at all, for he is the Son of God who . . ."

Hissing issued from the assembly, so loud that the man could not continue.

"Let him speak!" I shouted. "Let him sign his own warrant of death!"

The man Stephen turned his face toward me, then continued. "Did Pilate himself find any fault with Jesus? Did he not wash his hands of the blood he called innocent? I say to you that Jesus of Nazareth went to his death, indeed, begging forgiveness for those who screamed for his death and who would not even touch his tongue with water.

"Did you not see a man wet a sop with vinegar and offer it to Jesus in fulfilment of the words of David: 'They gave me also gall for my meat, and in my thirst they gave me vinegar to drink.' I submit again to you, sirs, that this was the Messiah, and that there is no redemption save in his redeeming, sacrificial blood."

He looked to me with a burning gaze. "To you, sir, I say, 'They are all gone aside, they are all together become filthy: there is none who does good, no, not one.' For all your strivings after perfection, your pompous strivings, you are no better in the sight of God than any heathen Gentile sunk in the depths of an idol-worshiping orgy, for you turn your back on God's only begotten son. No man is, in the sight of God, better than any other. It is only through Jesus Christ that there is justification, and you cannot buy him or earn him."

The words scorched like heated iron. Anger (or was it frustration?) smoldered within me. But I did not reply.

I did not move, nor did anyone else, as the man Stephen turned and walked untouched from our midst.

Early on the following day I was summoned from my lodging by messengers from Caiaphas, the high priest. I had previously informed Gamaliel of my new situation and assumed that the messengers located me through the teacher, an assumption which later proved to be correct.

We made our way through streets just awakening to the new day, and we did so with no word passing among us, so that my curiosity was whetted extremely by the time we reached his presence. He was seated alone behind a table in a sparsely and severely furnished chamber in the Temple precinct. He bade the messengers leave us and insure that we would not be disturbed.

I had, of course, seen this man on numerous occasions, but had

21

never before conversed with so exalted a personage. To have been summoned to his presence, therefore, filled me with mixed emotions.

"Rabbi Saul," he said in the tone of an examiner.

I bowed, and he bade me approach.

He was an uncommonly thin man of sallow complexion and sparse hair. His voice was rather high-pitched, and he spoke in sharp, direct, and calculated sentences devoid of any warmth or excessive wording.

"I will get directly to the point," he said, arising and beginning to pace with his hands clasped behind his back. "Yesterday in the synagogue of the Cilicians you withstood one Stephen, a potter and a follower of Jesus of Nazareth."

I nodded, but he was not looking at me nor, indeed, asking for a reply.

"You disputed with wisdom, and on one occasion you put down a rash attempt by the uncouth to put this Stephen to death."

I started to speak, but he began again.

"You are reported to be a man of unique ability, zealous of the law, and of unquestioned loyalty to Temple authority."

"That is true," I interjected quickly.

He looked sharply across at me, and I did not know then whether the glance expressed impatience at an interruption or investigation of a reaction. He continued pacing.

"You also have a powerful ally who vouches for the truth of those things reported of you."

A pattern began to form.

"Rabban Gamaliel is in agreement that your presence on the Sanhedrin might be mutually advantageous. What is your thought on such a matter?"

The suddenness of the proposition caught me off guard and I hesitated.

"Well?" he said.

"I would . . . be most honored, sir."

"Then it is settled. The man Stephen has been apprehended and is to be brought before the council tomorrow. You will be at the Chamber of Hewn Stone at the hour of trial. Jehovah be with

22

you." Thus abruptly he ended the audience and returned to his chair at the table.

Stunned by the cold brevity of it all I stood immobile for a moment, then bowed, turned and left the chamber.

I spent the remainder of that day in prayer and silent contemplation. The analysis of my situation was that my appointment to the Sanhedrin was not so much a reward as an expeditious act to placate the followers of the crucified Galilean. I would be seen on the council and remembered as the man who had stopped the mob at the synagogue of the Cilicians and advised trial by law instead of an act of violence. My "appointment" was itself a rude breach of formal tradition, for nominees to the Sanhedrin were supposed to undergo rigorous examination before they could be accepted. But Caiaphas ruled with an iron rod.

I did not like being used in so obvious a manner, nor did I like the curt, almost insulting fashion in which I had been approached. But my purposes were greater than those of Caiaphas, and I resigned myself to accept temporary personal humiliation in order to achieve the goals I was formulating for myself. With the power invested in me as a member of the Sanhedrin I could begin to throw myself with force into the cause of exterminating the insidious cult of the Galilean.

The man Stephen faced the Sanhedrin, seated in our crescent of benches, with the same disturbing calm with which he had faced the crowd at the synagogue of the Cilicians. I found my attention pulled to his almost glowing countenance, and my mind filled with wonder that he showed not the slightest indication of fear. Yet I knew that he had been dragged before us by a mob thirsty for his blood. He wore a white robe stained about the hemline and torn at one shoulder. There was a slight scratch above his right eyebrow, and blood had caked below it.

Caiaphas, resplendent and regal on his puffy cushion, sat at the front, next to his father-in-law Annas, former high priest and still a man of tremendous power among the Jews. Gamaliel sat on the other side of Annas and seemed to be less than comfortable, looking neither right nor left but frowning, and more at the mob than at the accused. I could only guess the things which were passing through the mind of my old teacher, for he was above all a man of consummate integrity; and this trial gave immediate evidence of being something less than a model of judicial decorum. For one thing, it had been hastily called; for another, fewer than half of the seventy-one members of the Sanhedrin were assembled in the tiered arc opposite the noisy mob whose palms itched to wreak their own justice. Stones would fly ere that morning had passed, and everyone, including the man Stephen, knew it.

Caiaphas cleared his skinny throat and said in rasping tenor, "Stephen bar Amos, you have been brought before this council accused of blasphemy against the most high God. We shall now hear testimony. Where are the accusers?"

"Here! Here!" shouted fiery-eyed rabble, rising and shaking clenched fists.

"Order! Order here!" shouted Caiaphas. I looked at Gamaliel and saw his eyes widen at the rude and disrespectful outburst.

"Two accusers and two alone are required by law," said Caiaphas. "Where are the two?"

"I am one," said the short, fat man whom Stephen had addressed as Malachi at the synagogue. He arose. "I heard this man declare that this Jesus of Nazareth would destroy the Temple and change the customs Moses delivered us."

"Yes, it is so," said another.

"He said those things and more," cried another.

Caiaphas raised his hand and shouted "Order!" Gamaliel looked at him as if in wonder as to why the high priest did not then clear the chamber.

Then a large man arose and faced the council, raising his hand for permission to speak. Caiaphas pointed a bony finger toward him.

"I am Caleb, your excellency," the man said, his fat jaws red with the flush of excitement. "That which is said of this . . . this blasphemer," he pointed a trembling finger at Stephen, "is all truth. Not once but many times he declared that Jesus of Nazareth could destroy our holy Temple, then magically raise it up again with a wave of his hand and then set up a new kingdom because he was the Son of God."

"Stone him! Kill him! Tear him apart!" came the shouts. I looked again at Gamaliel, who had turned and said something to Caiaphas. But the high priest leaned back and bent his head to a whisper from Annas. When the old, gray-bearded one had finished with him, Caiaphas called again for order, but not so forcefully as before. And the mob was longer heeding the admonition. When

25

the cries had given way to bitter murmurings, the high priest turned his face toward Stephen and pointed limp-wristed at the placid man.

"And what says the accused to these charges?" he asked. "Are these things so?"

All eyes turned toward the friendless prisoner, and he moved slightly into a position wherefrom he could see both council and assembly of accusers. His face was still as serene as it had been from the first and seemed, indeed, to take on a glow in the ray of early morning sunlight which fell upon it through a high window to my left.

"Men, brethren, and fathers, hearken!" he began. "The God of glory appeared unto our father Abraham, when he was in Mesopotamia, before he lived in Charran. God said unto him, 'Get thee out of thy country, and from thy kindred, and come unto the land which I shall shew thee.'

"Then he came out of the land of the Chaldeans, and lived in Charran. From there, when his father was dead, God removed him into this land wherein you now live. God gave him no inheritance in it, no, not so much as to set his foot on: yet he promised that he would give it to him for a possession, and to his seed after him, when as yet he had no child.

"And God said that Abraham's seed should live in this strange land and should be in bondage four hundred years to the inhabitants of the land. 'But I will judge the nation which they serve,' said God, 'and after that shall they come forth and serve me in this place.'

"God gave him the covenant of circumcision: Abraham begat Isaac, and circumcised him the eighth day. Isaac begat Jacob, and Jacob begat the twelve patriarchs. The patriarchs, full of envy, sold Joseph into Egypt, but God was with him and delivered him out of all his afflictions and gave him favor and wisdom in the sight of Pharaoh, king of Egypt, who made him governor over Egypt and over all his household.

"Now there came a famine over all the land of Egypt and Canaan, and there was great affliction, and our fathers found nothing to sustain them. But when Jacob heard there was corn in Egypt, he sent out our fathers first. At the second visit Joseph revealed himself

26

to his brothers and made his family known to Pharaoh. Then Joseph called for his father to come to him with all his kindred, who numbered seventy-five souls. So Jacob went down into Egypt and he died, as did our fathers, and they were taken back to Shechem and laid in the tomb that Abraham had bought for a sum of money from the sons of Hamor in Shechem.

"But when the time of the promise which God had sworn to Abraham drew near, the people grew and multiplied in Egypt, until another king arose who knew not Joseph. This king dealt craftily with our fathers and forced them to expose their young children that they might not live.

"At this time Moses was born and was beautiful before God. He was brought up for three months in his father's house; and when he was exposed, Pharaoh's daughter found him and raised him as her own son. Moses was taught in all the wisdom of the Egyptians, and was mighty in word and deed.

"When he was forty years old, it came into his heart to visit his brethren, the children of Israel. Seeing one of them suffer wrong, he defended him by striking the Egyptian. He supposed his brethren would understand that by his act he was giving them deliverance, but they did not understand.

"The next day he appeared unto them as they were quarreling, and would have reconciled them, saying 'Sirs, you are brethren; why do you wrong one another?' But the one who did his neighbor wrong thrust him away, saying, 'Who made you a ruler and a judge over us? Will you kill me as you did the Egyptian yesterday?' At this, Moses fled, and became an exile in the land of Midian, where he begat two sons.

"When forty years had passed, an angel of the Lord appeared to Moses in the wilderness of Mount Sinai as a flame of fire in a burning bush. When Moses saw it he wondered at the sight. As he drew near to behold it, the voice of the Lord came unto him saying 'I am the God of thy fathers, the God of Abraham, and the God of Isaac, and the God of Jacob.' Then Moses trembled and was afraid to look.

"The Lord said to him, 'Put off thy shoes from thy feet, for the place where thou standest is holy ground. I have seen the affliction of my people who are in Egypt, and I have heard their groaning, and am come down to deliver them. And now come, I will send thee into Egypt.'

"This same Moses whom they refused, saying 'Who made you a ruler and a judge?' did God send to be a ruler and a deliverer by the hand of the angel who appeared to him in the bush. He brought them out after he had shown them signs and wonders in the land of Egypt and in the Red Sea and in the wilderness forty years. This is that Moses who said to the Israelites, 'God will raise up for you a prophet from your brethren as he raised me up.' This is he who was in the congregation in the wilderness with the angel who spoke to him at Mount Sinai, and with our fathers; and he received living oracles to give to us.

"Our fathers refused to obey him, but cast him aside, and in their hearts they turned to Egypt, saying to Aaron, 'Make for us gods to go before us; as for this Moses who led us out from the land of Egypt, we do not know what has become of him.' They made a calf in those days, and offered a sacrifice to the idol and rejoiced in the works of their hands. But God turned and gave them over to worship the host of heaven, as it is written in the book of the prophets: 'O ye house of Israel, have ye offered to me slain beasts and sacrifices by the space of forty years in the wilderness? Yea, ye took up the tabernacle of Moloch, and the star of your god Remphan, figures which he made to worship them, and I will carry you away beyond Babylon.'

"Our fathers had the tabernacle of witness in the wilderness, even as He who spoke to Moses directed him to make it, according to the pattern that he had seen. Our fathers in turn brought it in with Joshua when they dispossessed the nations which God thrust out before our fathers. So it was until the time of David, who found favor in the sight of God and asked leave to find a habitation for the God of Jacob. But it was Solomon who built a house for Him.

"Yet the Most High does not dwell in houses made with hands. As the prophet says: 'Heaven is my throne, and earth is my footstool: what house will ye build me? saith the Lord, or what is the place of my rest? Hath not my hand made all these things?'

"You stiffnecked and uncircumcised in heart and ears, you always resist the Holy Spirit. As your fathers did, so do you. Which of the prophets did not your fathers persecute? They killed those who announced beforehand the coming of the Righteous One, whom you have now betrayed and murdered, you who received the law as delivered by angels and did not keep it!"

My eyes scanned the room when the last word had fallen from the tongue of Stephen. The assembly was as men half stupefied, totally speechless. Gamaliel, head slightly forward, sat motionless, his great mind grasping toward the dividing of truth. Caiaphas and Annas wore deep furrows in their faces, but they did not converse about the words. The Sanhedrin shifted nervously, and the mob opposite us began moving and murmuring and rekindling the flame of hatred with nods of mutual agreement. I felt a deep hostility, the whole truth of which I would not allow myself to face. The blasphemy dug deeply into my Pharisaic sensitivities, but the real hatred was a profound and overpowering jealousy of a man so completely at ease with himself and with his cause that he faced abuse and death in perfect composure.

A scream split the air: "Idolater!"

Men arose and fists stabbed the air.

"Blasphemer!"

"Stone him!"

"Kill him!"

The man who had first screamed tore frenziedly through the rabble and lunged at Stephen. A guard pushed him back. Another man, fists flying, rushed forward and was thrown back into the mob. Shouts rent the air and a sandal thrown from the crowd hit Stephen's head and fell almost at the feet of Caiaphas, who did and said nothing.

Gamaliel leaned forward and said something to the high priest, but he did nothing. Some of the Sanhedrin arose and stepped back as the clamor rose.

Men broke through the semicircle of Temple guards and struck the prisoner. Shouted curses pierced the air.

Stephen fell and picked himself up again. I looked at his face, his agitatingly tranquil face. Then he did a strange thing. He turned his eyes up toward the window and his words came as clearly as if there had been no tumult:

"Behold! I see the heavens opened, and the Son of man standing on the right hand of God!"

With that, the rabble surged forward and laid hold of him like a mad dog upon a rabbit. They pulled his hair and rent his clothing and dragged him from the chamber, but he did not cry out. Away they went with him toward the gate. I followed at a distance, wanting nothing more than to be rid of him and of the cursed, tormenting thing he did to me by being what he was.

As we swept along, the rabble pushed and kicked Stephen and screamed curses against him and his Galilean carpenter. The common herd fell in all along the way. I kept ever discreetly back, but never leaving the main body of tormentors. I wanted to see the man dead, to know for myself that the enemy of God could not prevail, no matter what demon of courage possessed him.

We passed through a gate of the great wall and stopped at the place of stoning. Stephen was flung bleeding and bruised against the great wall. As I clawed my way forward to see the execution, the leaders of the mob, recognizing me, charged to my keeping their outer garments, which they cast at my feet.

Stones flew then and beat into the flesh of the unresisting Stephen. A gaping wound opened beside his eye. He spun around from the force of the missiles. A purple mound rose on his neck, and there was a sickening crack as a large stone hit his teeth. Blood gushed from the multiple wounds, but the man never uttered a cry of pain. Nor did he, as some, curse his tormentors or beg for mercy. He looked up, and, in a loud voice, said "Lord Jesus, receive my spirit." Then he arose to his knees as the stones hit his body with renewed force. His hair was matted with blood and his white robe was crimson, but his voice was loud and clear as he said: "Lord, lay not this sin to their charge."

And he died.

In the months that followed, as a member of the Sanhedrin, I filled my hours with dedicated action against the accursed Jesus conspiracy. I allowed myself no time to think of anything else. So tremendous was my devotion to the Judaic cause that Caiaphas and the rulers of the Temple compounded my authority until the very sound of my name struck terror into the hearts of the followers of the crucified Galilean.

Feeling within that I embodied the strength of God, I laid waste the cult in Jerusalem, entering houses and synagogues unawares. With troops supplied to me by Caiaphas, I dragged forth men, women, and children to be cast into prison and tortured for heresy. Many felt the lash of my spiked whip as I drove them chained through the streets. Blood stained the cobblestones, and sounds of weeping filled the air. With each drop of heretic blood my enflamed passions cried out for the sight of more of it.

The example of my reign of terror brought me as much fame among the Legalists as fear among the cultists and my quarters were daily lined with informers eager to garner favor to themselves and escape the tribulation. Brother was aligned against brother, son against father, and the havoc wrought among the cult of the Galilean was so fierce that remnants of the persecution were forced to flee for their lives in all directions from our holy city.

Word came that those called apostles of Jesus were preaching and healing in various parts of the country. My zeal toward their extermination flamed bright as a result of my success in rooting them out in Jerusalem.

There was new spirit, a positive dynamism in me which I attributed to the power of God descended to my body in answer to ten thousand prayers. My renown spread abroad. I believed that, had I desired, I might have raised an army to follow me in the pursuit of my inspired mission. The scent of blood was in the air, and long-concealed hostility among Jews centuries oppressed burst forth like an erupting volcano. I was the symbol of that emergence.

I stood now in the presence of Caiaphas, or Annas, or any of the others, on equal footing. No qualms of nervousness possessed me in any presence. I could have stood boldly before Caesar.

Though I took no overt advantage of it, being satisfied to savor its contemplation, I felt that there was now some little fear of me in the mind of the high priest. I faced him now on equal terms, and, indeed, enjoyed such favor among Temple authority that my slightest whim was seldom refused. Some months after the beginning of my ascension I gained audience with Caiaphas and found him in a mood of deep concern. My request of him then was for papers authorizing an expedition to Damascus in Syria, for the purpose of rooting out, torturing, and bringing back in bonds to Jerusalem the Jesus cultists there. My particular target was an extremist named Ananias whose leadership among the blasphemers in the Syrian city had been disturbingly effective.

"Your request," said the high priest, his face more thin and sallow than ever, "is granted . . ."

"My thanks to you, sir."

". . . is granted on one condition."

"A condition?"

"The condition that you complete the task you set about to accomplish here in Jerusalem."

"Sir, the apostates are scattered abroad from this city. The insidious conspiracy is broken."

"Not . . . quite," said Caiaphas, the trace of a superior attitude in his voice. "There is one Joshua, a tanner, who has spread malicious falsehoods about myself and about the revered Annas."

His face searched me for some sign of weakening. Somehow he had found out about my previous association with the tanner and he was piercing at my armor with the ultimate test of my allegiance. I did not waver.

"My intelligence is, sir," I said, "that the man Joshua is of no consequence in the conspiracy."

"Your intelligence is in error. This very morning the man was seen near Herod's Palace in the company of a Cypriot revolutionary named Barnabas, probably plotting some additional mischief against the Temple authority. Bring me the man Joshua, and you shall have your papers for an expedition to Damascus." With that, he looked down at the parchments on his desk, signifying that the interview was at an end, and I bowed and left his chambers.

Now Caiaphas could have had Joshua at any time he had so desired, and he knew I knew it. The test was for me to bring the old man in to be tortured. The contemplation of this filled my mind with conflict and anger, which were in no wise assuaged by the time I had reentered my quarters in a large building, once an inn, just west of the fortress Antonia.

I found Gamaliel seated in a chair beside my table when I entered the room which served as my office. My immediate reaction was mild shock, for I had not seen the man except in passing since the day of the stoning of Stephen.

"I hope you do not mind," he said.

"Mind? That my old teacher should visit me?"

"You are busy."

"Not so busy that I cannot spare time for Gamaliel." I seated myself at the table. "What news have you?"

"News . . . no news. An old man has no news. You are the news." His eyes did not leave mine, and I suspected what things were on his mind.

"I? I do my duty."

"Yes . . . your duty."

33

"What is it, my friend? What is on your mind?"

"Do you not know, Saul?"

"You speak in riddles, teacher."

He looked down. He was very old now and very tired, and the ravages of time had taken their toll. The sparkle which had once been in his eyes had been replaced by a watery film.

I leaned back in my chair, still looking at his ancient profile. "You do not like the things I do?"

"The things you do are not for me to like or dislike. God judges, not I, nor . . ."

"Nor I?"

He did not reply.

I thought for a moment, then leaned forward. "Rabban, if you stood again before your classes and noticed one day a poisonous viper weaving its way among the feet of your students what would you do?"

He turned. "Now who speaks in riddles, Saul?"

"What would you do, Rabban?"

His gaze was steady. "I would advise my students to make no sudden moves, but to remain as statues so as not, however innocently, to incite the creature."

"What if you saw him on the robe of a student?"

"The example is not well taken, Saul."

"Why so?"

"Because you preclude the will of God."

"You mean the serpent might be there by divine appointment?"

"Or divine allowance." He arose slowly and went to the opposite side of my desk and leaned forward with his hands upon it. "My son," he said, "I have advised the Sanhedrin, before you returned to Jerusalem, and I advise you now of certain things. If this new doctrine is of God, neither you, nor your whips, nor your troops, nor your stones can overcome it. If it be of man, it will die. Now you think on this."

With that he turned and strode out of the chamber and left me more pricked in the soul than I had been when I had left Caiaphas.

That night, under cover of darkness, and shrouded in a heavy robe and hood, I made my way along the side streets to the house of Joshua. I knocked softly. When he came and made out my features, he paled and shook as one palsied and had to grasp the door for support.

"Are you alone?" I whispered.

He could not speak, but nodded his head.

I slipped in past him. When he had quickly closed the door, I threw back my hood. "Joshua," I said, "I must speak in haste and be gone."

His eyes were wide, and he leaned back against the door.

"Tomorrow at sunrise I will come here with a consignment of the Temple guard to place you under arrest. You will be taken before the high priest and then before the Sanhedrin for trial. You must at all costs deny this Jesus and disavow any relationship with the Cypriot Barnabas and the insurrectionists. Do you understand?"

"I cannot."

"What do you mean you cannot?"

His voice trembled. "I cannot deny the Son of God."

"You fool! Don't you realize I am offering you your life?"

"I cannot deny the Messiah of Israel."

"Your Messiah is dead! Crucified, dead and buried! He was nailed to a cross between two other criminals and he died! He does not reign in Jerusalem! He has not brought all nations beneath his feet! How can you be so blind?"

"He was dead and he arose and he ascended into heaven where he awaits the appointed time to return."

I came close to him and he turned away from my face. "I am talking about your life, old man!"

He did not turn nor answer.

"Then so be it," I said, and I spat upon his floor. "May God have mercy on your soul!"

I pulled my hood up and slipped past the trembling man and back out into the night.

The following morning just at daybreak I arrived on horseback with my troops and kicked down Joshua's door and dragged the old man forth, sending him sprawling into the street. As he slowly arose to his feet, he looked up at me. "The door was unlocked, Saul," he said, "as it has ever been to you."

I leaned down and grasped him at the neck of his robe. "Why did you not flee?" I whispered.

"I am an old man, Saul," he said, "and I shall not die denying the Messiah."

I looked with hatred into his eyes, then cast him down. "You fool! You misguided old fool!"

Joshua smiled. "I am not afraid any more," he said. "I am ready to meet my God."

With my letters of authority and my instructions in the methods of torture in hand I set forth in the company of ten men at arms for the city of Damascus. Passing through the gate in the great wall I did not look over at the stoning place. The execution of Stephen the potter returned to my consciousness, as it had on other occasions, but I dismissed it as I did any thought pertaining to the traitor Joshua. I had given the old fool his chance to escape his fate, and he had rejected it, so my hands were washed of him.

The heat would be intense upon the great stretch of wasteland which lay before us, and I did not relish the thought of the miles ahead, but I was strengthened tenfold by the implacable dedication I had shown in bringing for trial a man who had been as close to me as had Joshua. I knew that I had passed the final test of my faith in God and likened myself to Abraham, who had been ready to sacrifice his own son as a testimony of his faith in God.

Caiaphas, in a burst of charity which I did not fully understand, had seen to it that horses and pack animals were provided for our journey, but even this convenience did not offset the sore discomfort wrought by the relentless beating of the sun as we made our way past the Mount of Olives and down into the heat-cracked lowlands of the River Jordan. Rock-strewn passes gave way to hot and dusty

37

flatlands as our small caravan pressed slowly northward past Jericho and along the devious path of the river bed toward the Sea of Galilee, five days away by my schedule.

Each night we bathed in the waters of the Jordan and washed away the layers of dirt and grime which had collected on our sweat-drenched bodies during the day. Each night I stretched myself on the ground and prayed God to renew my strength for the mighty task he had set me aside to do.

I prayed thus: "O God of Israel, accept the thanks of thy servant for this great cause which was charged to thy servant when he had despaired of purpose and meaning in life. Grant to thy servant re-newed strength now in the total elimination of this apostate cult, and erase from his mind any human pangs of guilt deriving from those steps which must necessarily be taken in the accomplishment of thy holy mission."

Each night, and at frequent intervals in the monotonous travel of the day, these words were offered up to heaven. More than once I glanced around to see a member of the guard eyeing me with some perplexity, and on each occasion I would clear my throat as a device of concealment and restrain the fervor of my supplications. Outside of issuing the necessary orders through the captain, I did not speak to anyone, but stayed apart, my mind in relentless contemplation of the panorama of events which had brought me here.

Waves of heat smote us from above and radiated from the sand and stone of a vast stretch of wilderness which we crossed on the fifth day of our journey. I became faint in the noonday heat and swooned, but was caught by the captain and given water to drink so that I was able to press on toward the Sea of Galilee. At dusk, the first sight of that vast body of water renewed the spirits of us all.

We set camp by a small cove at the southernmost tip of the Sea, and having washed myself and taken my supper I began a stroll along the beach. The night was clear and the light of the full moon fell in silver profusion on the rippling waters. Finding a secluded spot beside a projection of tall reeds, I prostrated myself on the ground and had begun the saying of my prayer when the sound of voices brought me to my feet.

"It was across there," said a man, "near where the clump of willows juts out and . . ."

"No, it was farther north . . . about there. My cousin was among the multitude."

I parted the reeds and saw two of my guards wading in the shallows.

"He said the man Jesus got into a boat and was rowed out from shore and addressed the crowd," continued the second man.

"Was it then that he demonstrated his ability to walk upon water?"

"No, that was another occasion, when he stilled a great storm."

"Do you believe these things?"

"I only know what I have heard many times from many people."

"It is said that Jesus fed four thousand with a few small loaves and fishes."

"Five thousand, I have heard . . . and made the blind to see, and . . ."

"Stop!" I shouted, bursting upon them through the reeds. "Idolaters! Blasphemers! I have had men stoned for saying the things you are saying."

"We meant no harm, Rabbi," said the man who had spoken first, his eyes wide with fear.

"We were merely repeating that which is rumored in Jerusalem," said the other.

"Silence! Do you not know that I could have you bound and dragged back to Jerusalem in the very chains we take to Damascus?"

"We spoke no blasphemy, Rabbi."

"Blasphemy! Blasphemy! Get out of my sight and pray to God that he, and I, forgive you."

They bowed, then went hastily back toward the camp.

I trembled with the rage which had built up within me over the months past, shaking my clenched fist at the miserable, frightened men until all sight and sound of them was gone. I shook for a long while, and when I had regained some composure I again fell upon my knees and buried my head in my hands.

"O God, hold not the fate of the man Joshua to thy servant's charge, and strengthen me in the accomplishment of thy exalted mission." I raised myself up and returned to my tent but did not sleep that night for the strivings of my soul.

Setting out from the Sea of Galilee on the following morning, we encountered the steep, rocky headlands of the region of Gaulanitis, thence northward and eastward the way descended into another vast wilderness of forbidding, sunbaked earth known as the Tetrarchy of Philip. Three days of tortuous journey across this forsaken desert left my lungs choked and burning with the dust, my lips parched and cracked.

Less than a half day's journey short of Damascus we passed through a squalid, miserable little village called Mezze, from whose pitted pavement the heat of the sun radiated with renewed fury.

Within minutes outside Mezze we encountered an area of conspicuously craggy terrain, insomuch that our animals stumbled and balked, forcing us to dismount and lead them for some distance. The earth burned my feet and sent blistering rays up beneath my robe. The men cursed as they picked their way behind me.

We had proceeded thus for nearly an hour when the wind, which had been driving stinging sand into our faces, suddenly ceased to blow as though it had been shut off by the closing of a door.

I stopped.

There was no sound save the clicks of the horses' hoofs and the crunch of the gravel beneath the heels of the men, who seemed to take no notice of the vacuum, but continued on up the slight slope I had already negotiated. I breathed deeply, trying to fill my lungs with air which was not present. I looked up into the sky for signs of a storm, but there were no signs. No clouds loomed visible across the wide expanse of the heavens seared by the unrelenting fiery orb nearly straight above us.

Then, as if it had been a thousand thunderclaps, a mighty blast rent the air, and a light above the brightness of the sun enveloped us and sent me driven to the ground in terror.

Horses neighed and men cried out in shock, and I, blind and dumb, lay petrified on the bed of coals which was the earth.

A mighty voice burst forth from above, saying, "Saul, Saul, why persecutest thou me?"

And I, choked with fear, replied, "Who are you, Lord?"

And the voice said, "I am Jesus whom thou persecutest: it is hard for thee to kick against the pricks."

"Lord," I said, "what . . . what will you have me to do?"

"Arise and go into the city, and it shall be told thee what thou must do."

Then the divine audience ended. The great light left as suddenly as it had come. The hot desert wind returned. There was no more the feeling of the Presence.

I rubbed my eyes, but the scale would not rub away. It was as though I were looking through a thick haze, and the words of the mighty voice still echoed in my chaotic sensibilities. Crawling about like a dog half mad I could do nought but beg: "Help me! Help me!"

The horses had scattered at the sudden brightness and the loud sound of the voice, and the men groped and stumbled about in confusion. They had seen the light and heard the sound of the voice, but were wont to lose their minds at the wonder of it all. I could hear them moaning and calling out in shock, and it was a long while before their senses were restored so that they might attend to my pleas.

"Rabbi, what was the meaning of the great noise and the light?" asked one of me in an excited voice before he perceived my condition.

"I am blind . . . help me! Help me!" I cried.

I was lifted from the ground and led by the hand across the desert, falling, tripping, bloody of knee and elbow, through a gate of Damascus and to the inn of one Judas on the street called Straight, where I was to have been lodged. As I groped, arm outstretched, behind the soldier I was to have led triumphantly into the city, the sounds of those who had gathered to welcome me faded into awestruck silence. There were no plaudits, but whispers, as I passed with my disheveled escort through the midst of them and was abandoned on a pad in a dark and empty room.

41

For three days I neither ate nor slept, but endured the agony of hell. In strivings unspeakable all that I had been was wrenched out of me and replaced with that which I am. Blind to the world, I saw all the horrors I had perpetrated on the guiltless in nightmare succession on my inner eye as the Lord purged me with the fires of his chastening spirit. Waves of delirium came and went as my soul strangled on the innocent blood. My head split and my bones ached as my members warred against each other and bathed me in a sea of frigid, then scalding, perspiration.

The crushed skull of Stephen reasserted itself at maddening intervals between the tortuous progression of whip-scarred backs and sunken-eyed faces. The tears of wailing children rang deafeningly in my ears, and each pound of my heart was the thud of a rod laid hard across the prostrate form of a blameless child of God. I cried out for an end to it, but the end would not come. Hour fell upon anguished hour as the horrible error of my ways nailed me to the cross of my own shame. I screamed the accounts of my righteousness in the keeping of the law, numbering those things I had done without faltering, recalling the narrow path I had trod, but each phrase fell away, melted in the hot blood of the tortured saints of Jesus Christ.

Finally, when I despaired of life, the respite came. Nails of guilt were one by one removed and driven through the flesh of Christ. The pain of mental anguish gave way to the peace of God as the Saviour assumed the last tortures of my soul on the cross of my transgression. I had not earned it. It had come freely, when my guilt had been established irrevocably. I had cried out; then, in his own way, he had come.

Now in the final hours of my blindness a vision appeared to me of the man Ananias whom I had come thence to drag bound back to Jerusalem. I saw him healing me of my affliction. After the third day, this came to pass. Ananias did enter my darkened room, and he knelt beside my prostrate form.

"Brother Saul," he said softly, "the Lord Jesus, who appeared to you on the road by which you came, has sent me that I might be the instrument through whom you may regain your sight and be filled with the Holy Spirit."

He placed his hand upon me, and immediately the scales fell from my eyes and I could see. He smiled down at me as the face of an angel, and my heart was calm and warm in my breast and my spirit filled with thanksgiving.

"Can you stand?" he asked.

I nodded and, with his help, arose.

It was then that he baptized me . . .

Afterwards he gave me food and drink.

When I had finished eating I leaned back against the wall, and he, seated opposite me on the pad, with the light of the sun falling across the right side of his face and his beard and the top of his robe, began the blessed discourse.

"You have been chosen of God," he said, "to perform a sacred service of such magnitude that the mind of man cannot comprehend the end of it."

He spoke softly, but with an inspired authority which commanded my rapt attention. There was about him in generous measure that same aura of sainthood which I had seen in all the followers of Jesus of Nazareth.

"You are the chosen vessel to bear the message of salvation to the Gentiles and to such of the children of Israel as will hear—to men of all nations, both highborn and low. You must visit many lands and witness for Jesus Christ and suffer many things for his sake. Your life, from this moment forward, is his, and the things of the world and of the flesh must henceforth be subject to the things of his eternal kingdom. Your life will be one of perpetual self-denial in which your pleasure will be in him whose slave you are and whose chains shall bind you unto the end of your days."

The words of Ananias burned deeply into my soul, and I knew his words were the words of God. For hours I remained in close attention, not speaking and not at all times comprehending the vast implications of his words, humble, yet tingling with apprehension and sometimes shivering in fearful contemplation of those things which were made abundantly clear.

When his task with me was complete, he embraced me as the followers of Christ display their love for him and for one another, and departed, leaving me, as he said, in the hands of God.

Now God laid it upon my heart to make the first of many great journeys, for my mind was still beset with confusion on many points and I required solitude for the reconciliation. I was led of the Lord to go down into Arabia, there to prepare as did Moses, for mine was to be a journey of rebirth beginning on holy Mount Sinai, where God had struck the tablets with his law. Everything that I had been before lay in shambles at my feet; now with the help of God I would rebuild a life to be dedicated to the truth.

By day I earned my bread weaving in a small mountain village not many miles from the eastern arm of the Red Sea. I worked for a kindly man named Balar, with whom I was able to converse relatively well and to whom I was able to impart some of my slowly materializing message of Christ. Balar was a prosperous maker of tents, who sold his wares to the merchants whose caravans began at the coast and traversed the interior. He gave me lodging.

By night and during those hours of freedom granted me by the gracious Balar, I crossed that wide plain whereon had camped the children of Israel and ascended Mount Sinai by that which may well have been the path of Moses himself. My way led between huge boulders worn smooth by ages of wind and rain. At the very summit, where the air was clear and fresh, I found that which appears to be an immense projection of stone, piercing through and fully four times as large as any of the boulders, almost flat across the top, some three feet taller than myself, and five times as long. There is no doubt in my mind that this is the exact spot upon which the great God of Israel and of all men struck the tablet of Moses with the Ten Commandments. I climbed atop this projection and there, alone beneath the moon and the million stars of the universe, spoke with God—not as Moses had spoken with him, but through prayer and with my spirit open and receptive to his holy instruction.

For many months I availed myself of this communion with the Heavenly Father, until I felt my being fully cleansed of the error of my past. In every spiritual sense I was born again, and of the magnificent revelation of those days I may say that the summation of the revealed truth was that the law had never been intended of God to be a way of salvation, but a means of illustrating the need of salvation, which is attainable only through the shed blood of Jesus Christ, our Saviour, to whom be glory forever.

The long return trip to Damascus found me in wondrous contemplation of the succession of events which had brought me to that time and place. The hand of God had wrought order out of chaos and I remained in awe of it all.

Often, before the setting of the sun revealed the limitless reaches of his universe, a redness in the western sky brought to mind those days in my youth when, with my parents and sister, I had gone to the roof of our house in Tarsus to watch the crimson glow of the sunset on the snowcapped Taurus Mountains. The River Cydnus passed not far below us, and we had been able to see the grand ships, with their colored sails and banners, anchored or floating gently in the twilight breezes off the Mediterranean. The air had carried with it the muffled din of a great international city relaxing after the rigors of the day, and we had looked with pride upon it.

I thought of my father, the old Pharisee, a Roman citizen by his own cunning through trade, but a Jew to the core . . . my wealthy father, the maker of tents for the Roman army in Asia, but also the Pharisee who had instructed his son from the first in our special Judaic heritage. The Law . . . how it had lain upon and oppressed me . . .

I remembered that once I had badly cut my arm on the Sabbath.

46

I had lost a great deal of blood and I lost more while my father and my uncle were debating which oil might be allowed under the Law to be used on the Sabbath, and how far and in what direction one might walk to get it. I had hated the Law, but had not dared to admit it even to myself. As the years had passed I had put it on my body and on my soul and had worn it in racial pride and vanity like a heavy gold medallion, which strains the neck but reflects the status of the wearer.

I had worn my self-esteem in the shop of my father, in the class of Gamaliel and on the streets of Jerusalem, to a seat in the Sanhedrin, and then above the bloody backs of guiltless disciples of Christ.

These things returned to me again and again on the journey back to Damascus, and the cycle always ended with the boy . . . the boy I had seen in the Temple. My father, fulfilling his dream that I should be a rabbi, had taken me to Jerusalem to enrol me with Gamaliel. It had been the time of the Passover. We had gone to the Temple and I had seen the boy, no older than myself, addressing the elders. He had stopped and looked over at me, and his eyes had burned into my soul. The boy's eyes would not leave me on the journey back from Arabia.

Three years passed between my encounter with Christ on the road to Damascus and my return to that city from Arabia. My thoughts were of Ananias, and immediately upon my arrival I inquired along the hot and dusty streets as to his whereabouts. For days my search seemed doomed to frustration, until one morning an old woman in a marketplace directed me to the shop of one Asher, a goldsmith, who reportedly had been somehow associated with Ananias and reportedly had been the last to set eyes on him in Damascus. Asher, a tall, lean, black-bearded man with frightened eyes and unsteady hands, attired in a robe of multi-colored, vertical stripes, glanced furtively past me through the window of his shop, then motioned me to the rear. We parted curtains draped across an arched doorway and stood inside a small workshop cluttered with variously sized hammers, scribes, forming blocks, and bits of shiny metal spread out along a work table and hung about the walls.

"You are truly the Rabbi Saul?" he inquired, eyeing me no less suspiciously than had all the rest in that unfriendly, unconcerned city of thousands.

"Yes, I am Saul."

Moments of reflection passed, then he said, "If you are truly Saul of Tarsus, you must flee. The authorities are already aware of your presence in Damascus."

"What of Ananias?"

"Imprisoned in Jerusalem these seven months."

"Imprisoned?"

"Yes. The high priest Caiaphas sent others and took many of the brotherhood bound in chains back to stand trial before the Great Sanhedrin. I only escaped by the most fortunate act of providence."

"And no word since his arrest?"

"No, Rabbi. His last words were of Saul. His instructions were that, if you returned and found your way to me, I must implore you to remain outside the reach of Caiaphas during the time of this great persecution. The high priest is exceedingly wroth concerning yourself and has influenced the Jews."

"He knows of my conversion, then?"

"He knows that you deserted a mission which he authorized. Of what else he knows I am not certain, but you are a source of much embarrassment to the Jews and to Caiaphas as their leader."

He parted the curtain slightly and peered out into his shop. "You must return to the place of your concealment, Rabbi. Your life is at stake."

"I am not in hiding."

"But you must be. Your time is not yet."

"My time is now," I said. "Ananias suffers in prison for the sake of the Lord Jesus, and you would have me hide! I shall stand in the synagogue this Sabbath."

"But, Rabbi, I implore you . . ." He grasped my arm as I made to leave.

"Thank you, my brother," I said, laying my hand on his. "Thank you for your concern for my safety."

"It is the will of God, Rabbi; your time is not yet arrived."

I pulled away from him and left, the fires within me but fanned

48

by the warning and the news concerning Ananias. Two days later, the Sabbath, I stood in a synagogue of Damascus and expounded with all the fervor of a man unbound. The Jews looked, and murmured among themselves: "Is this not the same Saul of Tarsus who persecuted the followers of the Galilean? Whence speaks he now of redemption outside the Law?"

"I am the living proof of what derision lies at the end of the Law."

"Is that not blasphemy? How dare he set aside that which was instituted of God!"

"Blasphemy is rejecting God's son."

"God's son, indeed! A Galilean carpenter's son!"

"In whom was no spot or blemish."

"Blasphemy!"

"The sacrificial Lamb crucified for the redemption of sins unredeemable in any other way by man, who is not perfect, nor can be, nor can possibly buy salvation, which is not for sale, nor has ever been!"

They listened and they murmured, but they did not abuse me, being intrigued by the paradox I exampled. I came to be a sort of curiosity among the Jews, so that in the days following many came and some were converted and baptized. As in Arabia, I worked by day in a tentmaker's shed and by night brought the message of salvation to all who would listen. On the Sabbath I was in the synagogues where my training served me well. I thrived on the disputations, and, as Stephen, found myself continually reinforced of the Lord, so that no man was able to establish an insurmountable position against the truth.

After many weeks thus successfully planting the gospel of Jesus Christ and seeing evidence of its fruition, I was approached one night in my lodging by the man Asher, whose contributions, though anonymously offered, had been extremely liberal.

"The Jews lie in wait to kill you, Rabbi," he said, his eyes wide with fear. "They have secreted themselves about the house of Abel and lie in wait to pounce upon you when you go there tonight to speak to the brethren."

"You are certain of this?" I asked, my pulse quickened by the news.

"Yes, Rabbi. The plot was overheard by my wife this afternoon at the well of Sholar. You have incurred the wrath of the authorities, as I have warned you, and you have confounded them until you life is forfeit."

"They could have killed me at any time. I have done nothing in secret."

"They fear the people, Rabbi. You have a large following, but your work here is done, and you must do the prudent thing and leave so that you may continue elsewhere. I pray you in the name of Christ." The man's face bespoke the fervor of his concern; there was pleading in his eyes, and his brow was furrowed with the urgency of the moment. "We have provided for your escape."

I did not like the word "escape," but understood the wisdom of his words. "I will go," I said.

"Thank God," he said. Relief showed on his face, and he immediately set about to aid me in packing my things. "There are three of us, Rabbi, and we shall escort you outside the gate where we have tethered a horse and a donkey laden with supplies."

Within half an hour our group was proceeding with stealth through the darkened streets. No word passed among us, and we made haste toward the west gate. Within sight of it, one of our number, Jeremiah by name, turned and swept us back against the wall of a building.

"What is it?" I asked.

"There are men at the gate," he whispered. "Step out just far enough to look. There," he pointed, "at each side . . . and another next to the shop of the confectioner."

"What shall we do?" whispered Asher.

There was no reply, then Jeremiah turned to the other man and whispered, and the other man left hurriedly, slipping back into the shadows behind us.

"Where has he gone?" I asked.

"We have a plan, Rabbi, to get you outside the wall, and Nabar has gone for the necessary implements."

50

I did not inquire further, and the three of us remained pressed against the wall, hardly daring to move for over half an hour, during which time those lying in wait did not leave their posts. Then, at the sound of footsteps, we turned anxiously to see the man Nabar moving softly toward us with a large basket and a length of heavy rope.

"Now, Rabbi, if you will follow me," said Jeremiah.

We retreated for a block, proceeded south for twice the distance, then hurried back toward the wall again, stopping beside a shop which was apparently known to the two men. Immediately upon arrival there they darted into an alleyway behind the building and began bringing out wooden crates and scurrying with them toward the wall. Asher and I lent our backs to the task and, shortly, under the direction of Jeremiah, constructed a crude pyramid. The rope was tied securely to the basket. I was instructed to mount the pyramid with the basket, drop the basket barely through a watch window along the catwalk, and, while the three of them held fast to the rope below, to put myself into the basket, whereupon I would be lowered to the ground.

"God be with you, Rabbi," said Asher, and we embraced.

The other two men embraced me, and Jeremiah said: "The animals are tied beyond a mound just under a mile due west. There is food enough and water for your return to Jerusalem. God be with you, brother Saul."

My heart was deeply touched, touched as never before by an act of man. "Until we meet again, my brothers," I said. I mounted the makeshift ladder and took the precarious descent down the other side of the wall in the basket.

51

Upon my arrival in Jerusalem I went to the house of Joshua, but found the door locked and the windows boarded. Inquiring thereabouts I learned that no word had come of him since he had been taken away by the feared Saul and the Temple guard.

But the Holy Spirit impressed upon my mind the thought that this supposedly empty house would serve well the needs of a group still forced to secrecy. So I set a watch from an inconspicuous vantage point and waited. For six days I kept the house under surveillance, until at last one evening at a late hour I observed, within the space of an hour, the arrival of ten men. Each gained admittance after the employment of a cryptic knock.

When the street was empty I made swiftly for the door, used the same code and waited. Directly there was the sound of footsteps, and I determined that, when they stopped and the slightest opening was made, I would step quickly inside before there was a chance of recognition. There was the crack and a vague, shadowy form, and I forced the door back and burst into the room.

With that, the man who had been sent reeling back, shouted and advanced. There were footsteps in the room above.

"Have no fear," I said, extending my hand toward the man who was only barely visible to me. "I mean no harm to anyone."

The man stopped, and instantly there was a shaft of light through an opening in the ceiling at the left rear of the room.

"I am looking for a man named Barnabas," I said. "And I mean him no harm."

As the words left my mouth the form of a man dropped through the opening, and a lantern was lowered to his hand.

"Who wants Barnabas?" asked the man, advancing with the lantern held high before him.

"Saul, a disciple of Jesus Christ."

With the light falling now on both our faces and casting long, dark shadows, he peered suspiciously at me. I knew him, but he did not seem to recognize me.

"How do you know of Barnabas?" he asked.

"Do you not know me, Barnabas?" I asked.

He held the lantern almost to my face. "I knew a man once who looked and spoke much the same as you."

"Saul of Tarsus?"

"That was his name. He was a man who betrayed his friends and dealt horrible persecution to those who called upon the name of the one you profess to serve."

My eyes did not leave his, and with all the sincerity I could project into my demeanor I said: "Look at me, Barnabas, and know that I have been converted by the hand of God to a saving knowledge of Jesus Christ. Trust me and take me to those who stand fearful in the room above."

The big man stood immobile, inwardly debating what course of action he should take with me. He walked to the door and peered cautiously out into the street, then returned and said, "Come with me." He went back beneath the opening in the ceiling and called for a ladder to be dropped. When this was done, the three of us mounted the steps, and I found myself emerging into the room, dimly lighted now, which I had used as my own those years before. Now it was bare except for a long table around which stood those who had entered the house that night. I had no doubt that some, at least, were the Apostles, into whose charge Jesus had left the keeping of his church. They were common men, laborers by their attire, and by the look of their faces, men accustomed to the rigors of life. I stood before them as one on trial, their eyes examining me and an occasional murmur passing among them. Of them all, only Barnabas approached me, his massive frame being in a posture almost defiant between myself and the small door to the room below.

"Saul of Tarsus," he said, "what can you offer as proof that you have not come in trickery and deceit?"

I looked from him to the rest. "First, before I answer, brother Barnabas, may I . . . may I ask of the condition of Joshua?"

There was a low moan from the group.

"Joshua, whom you betrayed, is dead these three months," said Barnabas.

Another murmuring passed among the assembled.

I bowed my head at the news. "May God forgive me," I said.

"May God indeed forgive you," said Barnabas. "Now speak while we give you leave."

And then I began slowly to recount the details of my life from the setting out to Damascus to the present. As I spoke, looking into their faces, I was possessed of a feeling of warmth and love even though that which I saw was suspicion. I could not reconcile it, but it was as though being in their assembled presence was being in the presence of Christ. The emotion was a sublime spiritual security one must have felt in being physically near Jesus, though, of course, in a lesser degree.

When I had finished speaking, the change which I had hoped to bring in them was not wrought. One, a black-bearded man as large as Barnabas, arose.

"You speak of miracles and wonders worked in the converting of Jews in Damascus. Why is it that we have not been made aware of this by the disciples, and also made aware that you were to come to us?"

There was a nodding of heads.

"As I said, I departed Damascus in haste. No letter, even if one had been sent, could have arrived here before me."

"That would be so," said Barnabas. "Let us give him that. And, my brother Peter, you have been abroad in Caesarea much of the year past. All of you have been in your travels to various places, and it is possible that wonders could have been worked in Damascus without your being yet aware of it. Let us give him these things."

"Have you heard of a revival, brother Barnabas?" asked another. "You have been in Jerusalem these months. Has there been word of Damascus?"

"I have heard," said Barnabas, "that the number of visitors to our imprisoned brother Ananias has increased. And he himself is reported to have spoken of a miraculous conversion."

"But you do not have it from his lips?"

"No, it would be worth my life to go near the prison. The price on my head has been raised. But I also heard in the Synagogue of the Cilicians that a man claiming to be Saul the persecutor was preaching in the name of Jesus Christ."

"How do we know it is not all a trick engineered by the high priest to entrap us all?" asked the man Peter. "This Saul has used all manner of cunning and stealth in persecuting the brethren."

"But you have me, my brothers," I interjected. "Would Saul of Tarsus expose himself thus alone and unarmed if he were still the enemy of Jesus Christ?"

"He might if he were aware that the followers of Jesus are dedicated to nonviolence," said another.

"Yes, that is so."

"My brothers," said Barnabas, moving in toward the table, "please hear me. I may be somewhat more qualified to pass judgment on this man, for I met him once and spoke to him . . . here, in this very house. Whether he is truly converted I cannot say, since I did not see his conversion. But neither did I see the conversion of some of you, and . . ."

"It seems, brother Barnabas," said Peter, "that you exhibit an unusual eagerness to defend this man."

"I was about to say," said Barnabas, "that this man who stands before us now, this Saul, is not the Saul of Tarsus whom I met here those three years ago. And I see by your eyes that you question that statement. What I mean is that a great change has been wrought. I would swear to it. This man's speech, the reverent way

55

he refers to our Lord Jesus, his eyes . . . look into his eyes, my brothers . . . the calmness as he stands among us . . . I say Saul speaks the truth, and I recommend that, with the same love and forgiveness we received from Jesus, we welcome Saul into our midst." He extended his hand to me and I clasped it and thanked him. I was much impressed with his perception and with the benevolent spirit he displayed.

There was a discussion among the men, into which Barnabas did not enter. He stood beside me and seemed to await any decision with the same anxiety as I. Soon Peter turned and looked at him.

"Brother Barnabas," he said, "you have been rightly called the Son of Exhortation. We propose that a period of probation be included in any further discussion of accepting Saul into the brotherhood. If, in the space of a month, he has proven himself truly repentant of his former ways . . ."

"Our Lord asked no terms of us, brother Peter," Barnabas said.

"But we did not deal in persecution and murder."

"Degrees of sin, Peter?"

Peter scowled and I stepped forward. "My brothers," I said, "I would not have you in division on my account. I accept with deep humility the conditions set forth, and at the same time express my heartfelt gratitude to Barnabas for his trust and faith in me." I extended my hand to Barnabas, then to each of the men in turn. "And now," I said, "set me to the task at which I may best be of service to Christ."

It was the decision of that group to put me in the charge of Barnabas, since he had vouched for me and staked thereby his very status as the foremost disciple of Jesus Christ outside the circle of the apostles.

Barnabas had been a man of great wealth on his native Cyprus, a landholder of much power and prestige who had, upon accepting the Lord Jesus, sold all and lain the fortune at the feet of the Apostles. He was the most dynamic human being I had to that time encountered. Big in thought and spirit, as well as in stature, he went about the task of serving our Lord with all that was in him. He was truly filled with the Holy Spirit and was the type man with whom one knows he is headed toward a glorious goal. I had the feeling, the moment we stepped that night from the house of Joshua, that the world was ours to conquer for Christ.

It was cold as we made our way east through the shadowed streets, moving swiftly and cautiously for these were unpredictable times, times in which any follower of Jesus might be set upon under the cover of darkness and killed or put away forever. During the day, speaking to the crowds or in the synagogues there was not so much danger, for the number of the sympathetic had grown.

The hour was late when we passed through a small gate into a

57

walled courtyard which surrounded a modest but neatly-kept block home of the same flat roofed style as a thousand others. But there was here an orderliness uncommon and frankly unexpected as the abode of the big Barnabas. Though my new friend was a man of great character and quality he did not impress as one given to any element of daintiness.

In the courtyard there were trees and fragrant flowers and a winding stone path which meandered off the main walk and disappeared into the darkness at back. Bathed in moonlight it was perhaps the most inviting scene which had fallen into my view since I had left Tarsus those years before, and there was a moment of nostalgia for me as we walked to the door.

There was some delay between Barnabas' knock and the flickering of a light from within. He had spoken only a few words in crossing the city and had included no hint of his home situation, so I did not know whom to expect, nor indeed, until this moment, that I should expect anyone. I think I had pictured the man a confirmed bachelor, existing out of a small chamber in a rooming house somewhere near the center of the city.

When the door opened I beheld the most exquisite face I had ever seen. A girl of no more than twenty, with dark hair and, a face illuminated by the lantern she held, as gentle and smooth as the face of a child, stood before us. Black, frightened eyes looked from Barnabas to me.

"This is Saul," said the big man. "Saul, my sister Rachel."

I bowed, but no emotion displaced the fear with her. She stepped back, holding the door for us, then shutting it after a glance outside.

The house was not large, but it was as neatly kept inside as out, and the furnishings seemed out of place in that they appeared to be expertly made of the finest materials. A table to our left was heavy and solid and spread across the top with a fine linen cloth. There was a beautiful Persian rug, round, and about eight feet in diameter, in the center of the room, and, besides three chairs to my right, a smaller table whereon Rachel set the lamp. A large tapestry hung in the center of that wall. A door directly opposite the entrance led to a rear room. I had seen that there was an upper floor, accessible by an outside stairway which also led to the roof.

"Saul will be staying with us for a while," Barnabas said to the girl. "We will share my room."

The girl nodded.

Barnabas turned to me. "Have you eaten?" he asked.

"No, but I do not wish to be any trouble to you or your sister."

"It is no trouble," said Barnabas. The girl went through the rear doorway and returned momentarily with bread and wine and a bowl of figs which had come from one of the trees about the house.

This child moved with such grace and beauty that I had difficulty attending the words of Barnabas as we sat at the table. She was somewhat shorter than I and as delicate as one of the flowers of her garden. Her hair fell almost to the silken cord which bound her robe about her waist and it glistened in the glow of the lantern. She was, physically, as different from Barnabas as two persons could be, and I had some difficulty in accepting the fact that they were truly brother and sister. Later, Barnabas, perceiving a thought which must have crossed many minds, explained that his father had married again after the death of his mother, and this Rachel was the child of that second marriage. When both parents were taken disastrously at sea, the magnanimous Barnabas had taken the girl, more like a father than a brother, and provided for her every need. When he had accepted Christ and given all to the Apostles, she had come with him to Jerusalem.

I could see much of the Greek in the girl whom I found almost impossible to dismiss from my mind in the days that followed. Her beauty, which was more pronounced in profile, was but increased by the aura of mystery that surrounded her. She seldom spoke and, when she did, it was merely in response, softly, and with a cultured inflection. She was not happy, but she did not complain, at least not in my presence. She was like a sculpture come to life. Her nose and chin were classic, and when she brought her hair back and bound it tightly behind her head, allowing it to drop gracefully beneath the binding, she was, to me, woman as God had intended woman to be.

Striking examples were those days of the tribulation tempered with

59

love which was to be my lot throughout the remainder of my life. We were almost constantly with Peter, who never seemed completely to trust me, going with him in his rounds and learning much of the workings of the church. There were Sabbath disputations in a Synagogue of the Hellenists, to whom all things must be proven by logic, and the prayer meetings by night in various sections of the city. One of these latter is most clearly marked upon my memory.

Barnabas and I went under cover of night to a small house not far from the foot of Mount Zion. The area was a poor section of crowded dwellings wherein were found the unfortunate mixed with the rabble. It was an area not frequented by outsiders because of the reputation which had grown up about it as the realm of cutthroats and brigands. It was, however, a section wherein the feet of Christ had trod, because, as Barnabas had explained to me, it was to these that the Lord had directed the bulk of his effort. These were the hopeless to whom the Saviour had given hope, with whom he had broken bread and whom he had healed in body and spirit.

In the main room of the house, a bare and dimly lighted chamber, were gathered a group of about fifteen Jews, men with hard faces which mirrored lives of dissipation. These were men one might expect to encounter chained to the walls of a dungeon. Some bore the scars of horrible beatings; some were maimed with defects of birth, ghastly cripples who brought to mind at once those whom I had seen and from whom I had recoiled as a boy upon first setting foot in this city.

But there was not a doubt that these outcasts of society had come for a purpose. Barnabas walked to the midst of them and spoke.

"Now, my brothers, shall we bow our heads and pray. Our Heavenly Father whose love abounds to all, enter into our midst this evening that what we say and what we do might strengthen the cause of him who was crucified for all—thy son Jesus in whose name we pray, amen."

Barnabas looked over at me, for I had remained near the door, and extended his arm. I went to his side.

"Brothers," he said, "this is Saul of Tarsus."

There was some stirring among them.

60

"After a psalm," Barnabas continued, "Saul will speak to us of a conversion more remarkable than that of any man here. Brother Libni, will you lead us in a psalm?"

With that, a veritable giant of a man, a head taller than Barnabas, unkempt and marked by a deep scar from the corner of his left eye to his mouth, arose and began singing in a deep voice. Immediately, the brethren arose and joined in with such fervor that I restrained a smile. When they came to the part "Let the redeemed of the Lord say so . . . ," they all exclaimed "I say!" and Barnabas glanced at me and smiled. The psalm is long, but every word of it was sung with childlike devotion. When the psalm was finished they sat and waited for my testimony.

I had never faced such a group before, but any uneasiness I had experienced upon first entering the room had been put at rest by their manifest sincerity. I repeated the story I had told Peter and the men in Joshua's upper room. They listened in rapt attention, and, on inspiring occasions, interrupted with exclamations of the most unusual proportions. Some became glassy eyed as though entranced and uttered words unintelligible to me; others weaved back and forth and from side to side, seemingly enraptured by the flow of my words, which again came forth with inspired eloquence. Still others of the group merely sat and listened as did the cultured audiences in the synagogues. This was my first experience with the forceful manifestation of God in the early church at Jerusalem. When these strange things occurred I was intellectually aware of their unusual nature but undisturbed in the continuation of my testimony which was in no way hampered but seemingly embellished.

When I had finished speaking, a man no bigger than myself, but much older and scarred about the wrists and ankles, was moved to leap to the center of the room and emit such a flow of tranced utterances that I am certain an outsider would have considered him completely mad.

When he had poured forth all that had been laid upon his soul by the Holy Spirit, he returned, wet with perspiration and near exhaustion, to his chair. Then another, a younger man, came forth and interpreted the utterances, which were called "the gift of tongues." The interpretation was that the old man felt the presence of God in the peace which now possessed his soul. He had murdered his own wife and a man, and, in his later life as a prisoner had stolen from, and informed upon, those with him in bondage in order to receive special favor of the guards. He had lived with guilt for fifty years, and now was free from that bondage which is more punishing than shackles. God had forgiven him through the atoning blood of Jesus Christ, in whose name the old man rejoiced.

Those who did not respond in unusual ways to my testimony were later revealed to have been new members of this particular group of the church. The entrance of the Holy Spirit into their souls was manifest spectacularly after a tall, muscular, deeply bronzed man held forth with such impassioned eloquence that I was brought painfully to mind of the murdered Stephen. A common laborer, probably a seaman of some capacity, this man spoke with the ease and confidence of a trained orator. When he had finished the new members fell forward, prostrate on the cold floor and confessed their sins and praised God as being in their very presence. The power of Jesus Christ to salvation was thus manifest that night. As for myself, there was in me such unexampled exhilaration at the wonder of it all that my urge was to sing it in the streets.

Barnabas dismissed the group with a prayer, and after warm good-byes, he and I set forth down the darkened streets. We moved, as always, swiftly and in silence and had turned south on a narrow thoroughfare which twisted beneath a succession of archways, when the way some distance ahead was suddenly blocked by three shadowy forms.

Barnabas, seeing them first, grasped my arm and began searching for an avenue of escape. He pulled me around, and we had taken no more than three steps in retreat when, about the same distance behind, we saw other menacing forms advancing slowly. My heart was in my throat, for there seemed to be no alternative to violence. Barnabas leaped up to try to grip the lower edge of an archway, but could not get a grip. Then he pulled me close to him and whispered, "Stand behind me, and move at my signal." I nodded. By now both groups, at least eight in number, were closing in. They brandished sticks, and I had seen the glint of the moon on a knife blade. My heart pounded mercilessly as I looked from one side to the other, waiting for the signal from Barnabas.

Then he shouted "Now! Run!"

I leaped in behind him as he lumbered down the street in our original direction. The sight of his great bulk, robes flowing out like wings of some terrifying night bird must have given the three men a start, for they did not react immediately. Within five feet of them, Barnabas lunged out and, balancing his body on his hands placed flat on the street, bowled the three over like twigs in the path of an ox.

As I passed in the fray some hard object, a club or a sandaled foot, came hard by the side of my head and landed a crushing blow on my left shoulder. The pain was sickening, and I fell dazed momentarily against the wall of a building. Then Barnabas, who had sprung up, grabbed my arm and pulled me down the street just steps ahead of those in pursuit from behind.

The route we took led through back alleys, over walls, along the bed of a small stream, then back to the street which passed in front of the house of Barnabas. And all the while my shoulder throbbed, and my heart pounded with fear and the physical exertion. Where we lost the malefactors along the way I never knew, for, once started, I never looked back. When we had finally closed and bolted the gate behind us, we sank to the ground and leaned against it. My throat and chest burned, and the blood from my head had stained the shoulder of my robe. My shoulder ached so that I could hardly move it. "Who were they?" I asked.

Barnabas started to reply when a sound from the side of the house brought us both on guard, and Barnabas to his feet. I began leaning toward the shadows of a bush as two figures emerged from the trees. Stepping into the moonlight, they became the angelic Rachel and a young man whom I had not seen before. As they drew closer, the girl peered incredulously from one to the other of us.

"Barnabas . . . Saul . . . What is it? . . . What has happened?"

She ran to her brother, then, seeing my blood, knelt beside me. "What has happened?"

"Mark?" said Barnabas.

"Yes," said the young man.

"Mark, help me get Saul into the house."

"Careful," said Rachel. "His shoulder."

Holding my shoulder with my right hand, I grimaced as Barnabas and the young man raised me to my feet. I was half carried inside and laid on the bed in the rear room, which was Rachel's. Barnabas gently removed the robe from my shoulder, and Rachel came with a dampened cloth and washed my face and head.

"Can you move the arm?" asked Barnabas.

I lifted it slightly.

"I don't think there are broken bones," he said.

Rachel brought another cool cloth and laid it on my shoulder, and the young man lifted my head to a cup of water he had brought.

When they had done what could be done, they sat in chairs pulled near the bed. Barnabas smiled down at me, then suddenly turned toward the young man. "Saul," he said, "this is John Mark, the son of my sister Mary."

I nodded toward the fellow, who was dark and clean-shaven and, in the deep brown eyes and high cheek bones, definitely the kinsman of my friend. This was the first mention by Barnabas of another sister, and I assumed by the age of the young man that this Mary must be a daughter of the mother of Barnabas.

"We have heard much of Saul in my home," said John Mark.

"To the good I hope."

The young man smiled. "When the apostles came they spoke of you."

"I don't think Peter is yet convinced of my sincerity," I said.

"Peter is not convinced of anyone's sincerity," said Rachel.

"Now that is not fair," said Barnabas. "Peter is careful. He must be."

"These men," I said. "Were they a band of thieves, or . . ."

Rachel breathed a cynical laugh.

Barnabas looked at her, then back to me. "They . . . are assassins, hired assassins."

"Hired by whom?"

Barnabas did not reply.

"Tell him," said Rachel.

"We are not certain," said Barnabas, lowering his head.

"I am certain," said Rachel.

"Caiaphas," said John Mark.

"And Annas," said Rachel.

"We do not know," said Barnabas.

Rachel laughed again. She was displaying a side which, purposefully or not, had been hidden from me before.

"We are much hated by the legalist Jews," said John Mark.

"And by the Gentiles," said Rachel.

"This happens often?" I asked.

"Too often," said Barnabas. "May God forgive us."

"Us?" said Rachel.

"I do not like resorting to violence," said Barnabas.

"You had to defend yourself again?" asked John Mark.

"You should have seen him," I said.

"God forgive me," said Barnabas.

On the day following the altercation Barnabas left home early, insisting that I remain at the house and allow my wounds a time for healing. No manner of argument on my part would persuade him otherwise, so I resolved to dedicate the time to organizing a system of logic to be employed against the Hellenist Jews on the Sabbath following. The truths of Jesus Christ do not depend on logic but on faith; yet I had long since found that approaches vary with audiences, and I could not use the same procedure with the intellectual that I could use with the common laborer.

So I sat upon a bench in the shade of a tree, my mind off in the clouds and my physical pains as remote as the soft footsteps of Rachel, approaching from the house.

"Where are you . . . Arabia? Greece? Rome?" she asked.

I turned to see her smiling down at me, holding in her hands a small bottle of liquid and a piece of cloth.

"Strangely enough, I was right here in Jerusalem in a Synagogue of the Hellenists."

"Oh, I see. Well, perhaps you shouldn't be disturbed."

"No, no, no. Here, sit on the bench," I said, and moved over.

"I have brought oil for your shoulder," she said, seating herself beside me. "Can you stand the pressure of my fingertips?"

"Well . . . yes. Yes, thank you very much." I loosened my robe and she very gently removed it from my shoulder and applied a few drops of the soothing liquid. Very softly then, she began a small circular massage. "You have the king of all bruises," she said. "There must have been a lot of pain."

"Enough."

"Did you sleep well?"

"I have slept better. But I am grateful for your bed, and I hope have not inconvenienced you too much."

She laughed. "Not I. If anyone was inconvenienced, it was Barnabas. I took the upper room, and he slept by the front door after John Mark had gone."

"Oh?"

"Yes, I think he was still a bit uneasy about the men in the street."

There was a period of silence during which I considered this situation which I would, just four years before, have thought completely beyond the realm of possibility. I, a Pharisee of the Pharisees like my father before me, a member of the Great Sanhedrin and prime persecutor of the cult of the Galilean, sat in the shade of a tree, perfectly at ease, while a young girl of the Galilean cult rubbed oil on my back.

How strange, how beyond comprehension are the ways of Almighty God!

But this girl . . . Was she dedicated as her brother was dedicated? She did not radiate the joy of the other followers of Jesus.

"May I ask you something?" I said, the words coming automatically and even a bit surprisingly, as many of my words had lately come.

"I don't know," she said.

"You don't know?"

"Usually, when someone asks like that if he may ask you something, it is something personal."

"Then we will drop the question," I said.

"Now you have to ask it," she said.

I laughed.

"Ask," she said.

"It is personal," I said. "I was going to ask why you are not happy."

"Why do you think I am not happy?"

"You hardly ever smile, or talk. You seem to resent Barnabas' involvement with the cause of Jesus."

She put the cloth over my shoulder and returned the robe to its position. "There was a time," she began slowly, looking at the ground, "when things, at least things for me, were simple. Now, things are difficult. It is that simple, or that complicated."

I did not reply.

"I feel as though life is passing me by." She looked up. "You are looking at my world. I am twenty years old, and this is my world. There is no joy for me, and there once was, and that is why I do not seem happy."

"Does Barnabas know how you feel?"

"I haven't spoken of it, but he is no fool."

"Happiness lies in Jesus Christ. Do you pray?"

"I did."

"You quit?"

"I put myself to sleep praying every night for months. I prayed that God would send a way for us to get out of this place. We had such a wonderful life on Cyprus, and I have prayed we might return. I have even prayed that someone would come and take me away from this terrible city. But I gave up hope some time ago."

"Has it occurred to you that God has a reason for your being here?"

"You can grow old waiting for reasons to be manifest."

"You are very young, Rachel."

"Young and miserable."

"Throw yourself into the cause for which men are giving their lives. Sooner or later you will come to know that Jesus Christ is all there is and that there is no real joy outside him."

"You are not a woman, Saul," she said, looking over at me.

"Nor twenty years old. But I was once, and I hate the waste I made of life then."

"There has to be more in life than risking your life every hour of the day. Is that what God put us here for? I cannot believe it. The world is big, and beautiful, and things were not once as they are now."

"Since Jesus, you mean."

"Yes, since Jesus. I hate what he has done to us. I do, Saul, I hate it, and you can think what you will of me for saying it."

I looked into her dark eyes and knew something of the truth of her torment. I arose and took a few steps, then turned. "What do you know about me, Rachel?"

"Know about you?"

"Yes, what do you know about Saul of Tarsus?"

She looked at the ground again. "What they all know, I guess."

"Do you know that I was a murderer?"

She looked up.

"Yes, that is right. I was a murderer, a betrayer of friends, and possibly, at one time, the second most powerful Jew in Jerusalem. The world, you might say, was at my feet. There are worlds, and there are worlds, Rachel. The world is what you make it. The world can be a prison cell and, if Christ is there, a place of joy. Or a king, who has not peace of mind, can exist in a world of hell. Christ is the difference."

"Then I do not have him."

"Do you seek him?"

"Did you?" Her eyes flashed, then she lowered her head again. "I am sorry," she said. "I am not usually rude. You are a guest in my house. I don't even know what I'm saying."

I lowered my head and thought for a moment, then I looked at her. "Rachel, there are two ways in which those whom God has chosen may come to Jesus Christ. When the truth is made manifest, man may accept or reject it by his own free choice. If he accepts it, on faith, God welcomes him into the fold. If he rejects it, God is forced to wake him up and this way may entail ordeals undreamed of by a young woman. But the responsibility in either case is with man himself whom God has chosen. Once the truth is revealed, the choosing or rejecting is with man."

"It is all so simple with you, isn't it, Saul?" she said. "You are

a man. You come and go as you please. You have a life's work
to which you are dedicated. You are confident. Middle ground
does not exist with you."

"I have no time for middle ground. Men perish every hour of
the day, men without Christ, without hope. I have no time or place
for middle ground."

"Well, I have," she said. "And I feel sorry for anyone who
hasn't."

At that moment, someone called to Rachel from within the house
and she turned and arose. The caller was John Mark and he came
running through the back door of the house. His face was flushed
but wreathed in smiles. "Rachel, I have wonderful news," he said,
then he saw me. "Oh, Saul, how is your shoulder?"

"Much better, thank you."

"Rachel, James is here, in Jerusalem."

She did not respond.

"James, the Lord's brother?" I asked. I knew what James he
meant, but I asked in order to cover the awkward silence of the girl.
Even so, I could tell by John Mark's face that he perceived he had
interrupted some unpleasantness.

"Yes, the Lord's brother. And he will be with Peter tonight at
my mother's house. You will both come, won't you?"

"I would be honored," I said.

"Rachel, you will come?"

"I have not been feeling well," she said, picking up the bottle of
oil. "Please excuse me." She passed between us and went into the
house, leaving John Mark bewildered. He watched her until she
had disappeared, then he looked at me, and I lowered my eyes.

My first impression of Simon Peter had been that he had the largest hands I had ever seen. The fingers were thick and the skin horny and tough as ox hide. They were scarred by knife and splinter, burned by the sun, and creased and grooved by nets weighted heavy with tons of fish. His face was as bronzed as his hands, and black-bearded in an unkempt fashion which bespoke the rigors of the life of a fisherman who was also a chief apostle of Jesus Christ. His eyes were narrow, as the eyes of a man used to squinting in the sun, and the brows were slightly arched, with deep twin furrows between them. My thought was always that this was a man with scant allowance for humor and probably one to whom all men would have to be proven by their own merit.

"Saul," he said that night at the home of John Mark's mother, "this is James, brother of the Lord Jesus."

I had stepped inside the front door of another modest but well-kept home. John Mark stood beside me, and the man toward whom Peter had gestured stood to our left, in a doorway leading to an adjoining room. This man was tall, thin, clean-shaven and about my age, the late thirties. He had a prominent nose, but it did not detract from his appearance. Rather, it enhanced it, for he was raw boned, manly, and keen of eye. There was strength in his mien and in the grip of his hand. His eyes were pale gray, strong, yet capable of tender understanding.

"Welcome, brother Saul," he said, in words whose force told of their sincerity. "Barnabas has spoken great things of you."

I smiled and bowed. "Barnabas is often too generous," I said. I was magnetized by this man, who was undoubtedly the most prepossessing male I had ever met. There was a magnetism about him, which extended far beyond his personal appearance. He was magnetic, much as his brother must have been to have drawn people by the thousands to be held then by the dynamism of his message.

"Ah, Mary," said Peter, looking past James.

James stepped aside and held out his hand to a middle-aged woman of gray-streaked hair and dark complexion. Wide-faced and large-boned, she was, I knew, the sister of Barnabas.

"Mother, this is Saul," said John Mark.

"Welcome to this house, sir," said the woman as I bowed. "Peter, you asked me to inform you when Barnabas arrived. He is in the meeting room."

"Thank you," said Peter, and he led us behind Mary into this room, which, like the room of the previous night, had been provided with a circle of chairs. Barnabas was storing some parchments inside a cabinet which stood next to the door through which he had entered.

"Saul," he said, looking up. "This is a wonderful surprise. You have met James?"

"Yes. We were talking when you came in."

"Good. And the injuries?"

"Much better, thanks to your sister."

"Where is Rachel?" asked Peter.

"She could not come," said John Mark. "She was ill this morning."

I made a point of looking at Barnabas. He looked up from his work, then down again.

"It is nothing serious," I said. "A headache."

"She is alone?" asked James.

"I leave her alone too much," said Barnabas, arising.

"That is something of the purpose of our being here," said Peter. "Shall we pray, and then have a few words before the others arrive?"

We bowed.

"Lord God, we stand before thee with thanksgiving for the multitude of blessings bestowed upon us. In the trying days ahead continue thy presence in our midst so that we may be able to withstand the fiery darts of the wicked. In the name of our Saviour Jesus Christ, amen."

We seated ourselves, and Peter stood in our midst. He spoke hoarsely, almost painfully, and he seemed drained of the vitality I had seen in him in Joshua's upper room.

"My kinsmen in Christ Jesus," he said, "it is on a subject of some delicacy that I speak to you tonight." He bowed his head as though searching his fisherman's mind for the right words to express that which seemed to lie so heavily upon him. "As you know, the church prospers in all the regions round about. James has just returned from a second visit to Samaria where he found the brethren multiplying. And this is the rule rather than the exception in the outlying areas, as reported to us by Andrew and the others. This is good, and we praise God for it."

He paced a short distance, head down again, then looked up.

"But the fact is that Jerusalem itself is not enjoying the same optimistic climate. And this is no reflection on the disciples, but rather of the concerted opposition centered with the high priest. The Hellenists have his ear continually, and they are much disturbed by the words of brother Saul, who, incidentally, has proven himself to me beyond the shadow of a doubt. But it seems that the truth Saul brings is enjoying too much success, and this is causing consternation among the leaders. Saul represents all that is failure in legalist Judaism and all that is triumph in Jesus Christ, and this is more than the legalists, particularly the high priest and the Great Sanhedrin, can tolerate or afford to tolerate."

He turned to me. "We have news, Saul, that except for the intercession of Rabban Gamaliel, you would have been taken or killed days ago."

73

The news stirred my heart with fear, but much more with a re-kindling of the love I had always felt for my old teacher.

"In short," Peter continued, "we want no harm to befall you. And we also cannot afford at this time to suffer increased persecution in Jerusalem. The atmosphere now is charged with hate and fear, and it is but increased by the presence of a living symbol of legalistic failure walking the streets and speaking in the synagogues. So it is with deep regret that we must ask brother Saul to leave Jerusalem. I am sorry."

The words hit me hard, but I summoned up what resources I possessed to hide my feelings. My eyes did not leave the face of the big apostle, whose sympathy was apparent. He knew what it was to burn with the spirit of Jesus Christ and be unable to give vent to it. This request, which I knew had come from all the apostles, and therefore from God, would mean my leaving Israel at least until the passions of the authorities toward one whom they considered worse than a traitor had cooled. It could be an exile of many years. Peter knew it. They all knew it. Though I hated it, I knew it was the only course.

There were services that night, but I did not speak and heard only parts of what was said. Barnabas and I returned in silence to his home, and I began at once to gather my things. The obvious choice for me was to return to Tarsus. The advantages of that city outweighed those of any other. There were painful memories there, but I had a house standing empty in a city I knew, a city large enough to enable one to work for Christ without arousing too much attention. I would attach myself to one of the many tentmaking establishments to earn my livelihood. I would witness for Christ in whatever way he might direct, thinking always of that future time when I should again be permitted to sound forth the Gospel to the great masses of my fellowmen.

I had almost completed my packing when I looked up to see Rachel standing in the doorway to the room I shared with Barnabas. He had gone out to arrange for a donkey to take me to Joppa where I would book passage for Tarsus.

I looked at Rachel.

"Will we see you again?" she asked. Her eyes were red, and their long black lashes glistened with moisture.

"God willing," I said.

"Where will you go?"

"Back to Tarsus."

"Do you have anyone there?"

"A sister, and the sister of my father." I continued putting things in the cloth bag.

"Saul . . ."

I looked up.

"Saul, take me with you."

I did not reply. She came closer.

"Please take me with you. I will not be in your way."

"Rachel, Rachel . . . Don't you realize I am running for my life? Even if I could entertain such a thought, you would be risking your life also just being in my company."

"I don't care. I am dying here."

"It is out of the question."

"Saul, look at me. I beg you to take me away from this place. Are you going to Joppa? Leave me at Joppa. I beg you."

"Rachel, be sensible."

"I beg you, Saul."

"It is out of the question. Believe me, one day you will know."

She backed away. "No middle ground," she said. "No middle ground."

"Believe me, Rachel, it would be wrong. Give yourself to Christ. That is the only way you will be happy."

"You mean die for Christ, do you not?"

"If that is to be."

She did not say anything more, but stood and looked at me until I had finished. As I passed by her I stopped. "Give yourself to Christ, Rachel. He wants you, and he needs you."

She looked at me, but her lips were tight and her eyes were filled with bitterness.

Of the lonely eight years following I have little of consequence to say. My sister and my aunt were as strangers, rejecting any word of the Gospel and closing the door of their home to me. This period was truly the low point of my life as a disciple of Christ, and I am certain it was decreed by God that this should be so. My memory was tortured by those things I have set down here, but out of it all there slowly emerged a strengthening of character which was to see me through the days of trial which lay ahead. I lived alone in the house of my late parents, and, for my daily bread, did indeed secure a position with a tent merchant named Joab, whose business was so successful that I was but one of many employees, both Jew and heathen, engaged in the weaving of cloth. I did carry on a witness for Christ among my fellow workers and during whatever additional occasions presented themselves in this period, but by and large my ministry was passive and my life one of relative solitude.

A letter from Barnabas during the first year of my exile informed me, to my inexpressible sorrow, that Rachel had left him, departing while he was away, with no more explanation than a short note containing none of her plans or destination. By the tone of Barnabas' communication I knew that this had been an ordeal for him and one which burdened him with tremendous guilt. If the man knew anything of my brief encounter with the girl that final day he gave no indication of it, so that I supposed it would be another of those regrettable things to be forever closeted in my heart.

But my love for Christ increased with the passage of time, as indeed it must when one is driven to the blessed realization that the Saviour must be his all. This was one of the truths which was drawn into my mind by the Holy Spirit during the hours of prayer and silent strivings. The love of Jesus Christ is sufficient to enfold us all.

My correspondence with Barnabas was an occasional but a blessed thing which continued throughout the eight year period. He spent a year in searching for Rachel, and during that time I had no word from him. But when his mind was reconciled to the fact of her loss, he returned to his discipleship with fervor and kept me apprised of the tremendous progress of the church and of the acts of the apostles. There was very little I could report to him, but the highly informative letters he sent to me were eagerly anticipated and reread with enthusiasm.

Perhaps the foremost of these letters was one recording an event of paramount importance in the history of the world. The apostle Peter, journeying in Joppa and staying at the house of one named Simon, had had a vision of a great sheet descending from heaven. On this sheet there had been collected many beasts, reptiles, and birds, and a voice had come to Peter saying: "Rise, Peter; kill and eat." Peter had said; "No, Lord; for I have never eaten anything common or unclean." But the voice had come back again: "What God has cleansed, thou must not call common." This had occurred three times, and then the sheet had been taken up into heaven.

Now just shortly before, a righteous Gentile, a centurion named Cornelius, of Caesarea, had also had a vision and had been told to send men to Joppa to fetch Peter to his presence. When Peter had awakened from his vision, the envoys of Cornelius had been at the gate of the house of Simon asking if Peter were there. Peter had then revealed himself to them, and, on the following day, had accompanied them to the house of Cornelius in Caesarea. At this house, with many Gentiles gathered, Peter's mind had been made aware of the meaning of the vision: that all men of whatever race are clean in the sight of God if they fear him and do that which is right.

Then Peter had expounded the gospel, and the Holy Spirit had descended upon Cornelius and his family, and they had spoken in tongues and extolled Almighty God. Peter had then baptized them and had received them all into the fellowship of the church of Jesus Christ without the formality of circumcision.

The importance of this event cannot be overestimated, for it revealed the will of God in respect to the equality of mankind redeemed. And, more personally to me, it opened the door to the vast undertaking which was to consume the remainder of my life.

Very soon after the baptism of the Gentiles, the Lord moved in a mighty way in the prosperous city of Antioch in Syria. This city is an integral part of the commercial workings of Rome, being vital in both land and sea trade. So vital is it, in fact, that it is designated the eastern capital of the Roman Empire. Its main street, four miles in length, is lined with mansions. And, with a population of half a million, it is the third largest city of the Empire. The people, surrounded by luxury, had fallen into revelry and debauchery, but even here, an extensive revival had broken out among the Gentiles, and I now take a degree of consolation in the fact that this revival was begun by fugitives driven there by the horrible persecution visited upon Jerusalem by Saul of Tarsus.

In due course, the apostles, mindful of the significance of the outbreak of enthusiasm for Christ, sent Barnabas to oversee the endeavor, I being made aware of this in another letter from my friend. Within a month of receiving the letter I returned home one afternoon from work to find Barnabas himself standing at my door.

Is it possible to put into words the joy, the positive elation one feels at the first glimpse in years of a cherished friend? I think not, for love in Christ is beyond the full comprehension of man. I do know that tears welled up in my eyes, and I embraced the big man unashamedly.

We supped together that night, and I ate as I had not eaten in years. Barnabas, noting my buoyant spirits, was moved to laugh, and I vow that was the first laughter within those walls in over a decade. We laughed much and exchanged stories. It was not until later, seated on the roof, that he disclosed the true and serious purpose of his visit.

"You are needed, Saul, in Antioch," he said. "The awakening is more than I am capable of handling alone, and I have the authority of the apostles to ask your aid."

"Then my time has arrived at last," I said, looking past him at the moonlight on the bay of the Cydnus.

"I believe that it has," he said.

"Praise God."

"Praise God for preserving you to this task," said Barnabas.

I stood and walked to the edge of the roof, still looking out past the hundreds of squat block houses toward the bay. "If you only knew how many hours I have spent in prayer for this moment . . . how much loneliness I have endured that this might come to pass."

"The ways of God," he said.

"Indeed, the ways of God." My thoughts traveled back over the long, gray years to that night I had not been able to forget. And though I did not know what pains it might evoke in my friend, I could not longer restrain the question. "Has there been any word of Rachel?"

"None."

"Did she . . . have money, friends, any means of . . . keeping herself?"

"She borrowed money from John Mark on the pretext of buying a robe for me. I had mentioned seeing one . . . an expensive one which caught my fancy."

"But what would she have done? Where would she have gone?"

"I do not know. And I have exhausted every avenue of inquiry. Unless she secreted herself, she did not join any caravan leaving Jerusalem. And yet I cannot believe she would set out alone. It is the most baffling mystery."

"Did you go to Cyprus?"

"Immediately. It was my first thought that she had gone back to the island . . . She loved Cyprus. But no one had seen her. I have looked in every conceivable place. I look at every woman's face on every street I travel. I have written scores of letters and have given her description to the authorities in every place I have been."

My fingernails dug deeply into the palms of my hands as he spoke. The torture I had first endured at word of her leaving was back with me tenfold and I could not tell him of it, of what the child had meant to me and of the piercing thorn of guilt which tormented my flesh. I could have taken her at least to Joppa and found a place for her. I would have done as much for a repentant murderer.

"I have awakened from nightmares of her at the mercy of some depraved highwayman," he said, "and I have kept myself sleepless night after night so that the dreams would not come. This Antioch commission was given to me at my own request. I thought that I might be able to forget if the task were big enough . . . and it is. It is too big. That is why I have come to you."

"I am ready, my friend," I said, "to go to Antioch—or to any other place on earth where the Lord might direct."

Our success in Antioch was spectacular. The sensual place was turned upside down for Christ.

Barnabas and I threw ourselves completely into the task. Never had I known such personal satisfaction, such inner peace. The Lord added thousands to our number. Within a matter of months Antioch had become headquarters of the church of Jesus Christ. So powerful was the movement that the heathen bestowed upon us the name "Christian," a derisive title to them, but a name in which we gloried and shall glory forever.

The good news was spread to the regions thereabout and in due course the most far-reaching proposal of all for accomplishing the Lord's purpose came to realization. This was the inspired resolution to send forth to the heathen world at large a mission for Jesus Christ. Under this plan, a team of the members' choosing would set out from Antioch toward the unreached millions of the Roman Empire. My prayers were constant and fervent that I might be chosen as part of this mission. The work which Barnabas and I had set about to do in Antioch was done, and I felt that our experience and whatever special talent we might have possessed in this regard qualified us for further work of a similar nature. My energies, charged by God, were so seemingly boundless that I found it almost impossible to relax, and the wasting of a single second of time was a painful thing to me. I needed new worlds to conquer, and so I prayed.

During this time the monstrous Herod Agrippa was visiting unspeakable persecution on the Christians in Judea. He killed James, the brother of John, and hacked a bloody path through the body of Christ. This but increased my zeal for the Lord and the fervor of my prayers to be used according to his will.

So I fell to my knees and praised him before the church assembled when I was chosen for the missionary task, and my joy was but increased by the fact that Barnabas was chosen to be my companion. During the succeeding days of planning, Barnabas and I were sent on a mission of mercy to Jerusalem. We took food and supplies from the Antioch church to the brethren in the holy city who were suffering a killing famine.

It occurred to me while we were there that expediency might be served in our forthcoming missionary venture if we added a third party to arrange details of travel while Barnabas and I preached the gospel. My friend agreed, and we approached his nephew, young John Mark, who had impressed me strongly in the few short days I had known him.

Whenever I thought of Rachel I thought of the boy and of his enthusiasm for the Christian movement and of his youth and stamina. The experience would be invaluable if he intended to give his life to the Lord.

John Mark accepted over the misgivings of his mother Mary.

"He is a man, sister," Barnabas said. "It is time you recognized that fact."

The woman cried, her son being all she had in the world; but she knew that her brother was right and saw what the experience could mean for John Mark. So she gave her blessing.

One month later, the three of us set out, under fair skies and before a friendly breeze, across the narrow stretch of Mediterranean between Seleucia, the seaport of Antioch, and the island of Cyprus. The itinerary would include Cyprus, then whatever regions God might indicate as we traveled. The plan of journey was largely the work of Barnabas, who still entertained some hope of finding his sister on the island. I was no less hopeful than he.

We sailed aboard a Greek vessel called the "Swan of Salamis," and arrived the same day at that thriving seaport. Salamis was the home of Barnabas, and the positive exuberance which the man displayed as we set foot upon the dock left no doubt as to the fact that to him this was a joyous homecoming.

He gestured and spoke in detail of the points of interest as we passed by the rows of merchant ships, their naked masts jutting skyward like trees in a winter forest. We took a narrow winding street to the top of a slight rise from which, as purposed by the big man, we could view much of the city.

He proceeded to point out to us the sights, which he recalled with fondness, making a wide sweep of his arm toward a richly-endowed spread of green land far to the south and west. This had been his property, and a house whose glistening walls shone through a stand of trees in the center of the section indicated had been his and Rachel's.

It was no cause for wonder that the girl had spoken with such longing for return. There seemed to be nowhere in view the press and bustle of Jerusalem, but rather a clear and stimulating atmosphere capable of producing happy sons and daughters. There was even a certain gaiety of spirit evidenced in the varicolored roofs on the houses which spread profusely before and below us.

We passed the night at an inn not far from the point from which we surveyed the city. Early the following morning we went to friends and former business associates of Barnabas, none of whom could shed any light on the whereabouts of Rachel, or Ephraim, the son of Joshua.

One, however, offered us the use of his warehouse and a certain period of the day in which to bring the gospel to his employees. This warehouse was just across and down from the dock at which our ship had berthed. At midday, with at least a hundred men squatting, standing, or stretched out at our feet, we held the first missionary service for Christ, that hour adding forty-seven souls to his church.

Each day for two weeks we spoke at midday in the warehouse, and on the Sabbath met with the Jews in the synagogue. The one place echoed with the ring of voices in word and psalm, and the other knew intellectual disputation. Our evenings were spent in the homes of the converted or of the friends of Barnabas, and the spirit of Christ was manifest with power and glory. The curious of every level came and heard and came again.

John Mark, who knew many of the same people as Barnabas and who also knew the island, having traveled extensively with his uncle, fulfilled his function admirably in arranging our schedule in Salamis, and also, when the time came, in presenting for our approval, an itinerary for evangelizing the main cities of Cyprus. His route would take us along the southern coast to the extreme western point, the city of Paphos, where we would debark for the coasts of Asia.

So at the end of two weeks we set out south and west on foot, our confidences bolstered by the success in Salamis and our spirits buoyed by the encouragement of the friends of Barnabas. Days of clear blue sky and a warming sun saw us wind our way past the bays and inlets of the southern coast, through ancient Chittim, which is said to have been founded by Kittim, the great-grandson of Noah, and alongside the living yellow fields of grain sickle-harvested by the farmers and their women.

We stopped now and again for water, or to ask a direction, or simply to pass the time of day with a man tossing grain high into the air to separate the wheat from the chaff, or with a farmwife goading a stubborn ox turning a grindstone. And each time I saw the goad with its sharp pricks I thought about the words of Jesus to me the years before on the way to Damascus. We always spoke of Christ to those we met along the way, sharing the good news with hearts we found. They were, almost without fail, eager to absorb the words of hope and promise we brought.

At night, we often slept with shepherds tending fat-tailed sheep along the hillsides. We shared food from their goatskin pouches, trading stories of Christ for tales of pastoral gods. Bidding them good-bye on the following mornings, we took strength at the thought that seeds of the gospel had been planted, to be watered by the Holy Spirit.

For days we traveled, past groves of gnarled olive trees and well-tended vineyards, down dusty roads traversed by oxcarts piled high with brushwood, at times picking our way with our staves over rocky passes and stopping to rest beneath the sheltering boughs of trees in grassy meadows often stretching to the edge of the blue Mediterranean.

At city and village we paused and spoke the good news of Christ to all who would listen, baptizing such as were added to the faith, and sharing the meager living we earned by the strength of our bodies. We kept nothing for ourselves save that which was necessary for the physical needs, and we fed our souls with the bounty of God's riches in the conversion of his children.

On the sixty-first day after setting foot on the island of Cyprus we departed the town of Curium, whose chief features had been magnificent baths and a theater located atop cliffs towering over the rock-strewn shores of the sea.

Because of some difficulties we had encountered among the Roman authorities, our successes at Curium had not been as marked as they had been elsewhere, and our spirits were not as elevated, especially those of John Mark, whose moods, I had noted with some concern, were given at times to unconcealed fluctuations. I loved the youth, but there were moments when he displayed something less than his initial enthusiasm and that which was warranted by the unexpected succession of virtually unchallenged victories for Christ. I was never quite sure of his total reliability.

Two days toward Paphos, having refreshed ourselves at a brook in the hills, we were adjusting the small packs we carried on our backs when the wind carried to our ears the sound of raucous laughter. I dismissed it at first as the playful cry of children in the lowlands nearby, for, as I have said, these are a happy people. But farther down the curving road we reached a point above a wide, grassy plain whereon stood an enormous edifice from which came the laughter. It was a pillared structure, of gleaming marble, in an architectural style which I was later to find abounding in Greece. That is, it was rectangular in shape, long, and a perfect complement of verticals and horizontals. It was breathtaking for its splendor and so unexpectedly incongruous with the untouched wilds surrounding it that I stood momentarily as one entranced.

"The Temple of Aphrodite," said Barnabas solemnly.

"The goddess of love, beauty, and fertility," added John Mark. "She was said to have been born of the foam of the sea at Paphos."

"It is magnificent," I said.

"Magnificently corrupt," said Barnabas.

"Let us go on," said John Mark.

"But wait," I said. "I have never seen anything like it."

"Nor should you. Nor anyone," said Barnabas. "Mark is right. We should move on."

But I paid no heed, stepping off the road toward the thing as though pulled by some irresistible urge. There were protestations from behind, but then my companions followed at a distance. Drawing close to an open portal, I moved to a position from which I could observe the now piercingly disturbing tumult from within, and I beheld a sight which was wont to make me ill. Men and women, in a pagan rite of worship, were involved in an orgy of unspeakable proportions. Scores of human beings, sunk in depths of depravity reminiscent of the licentiousness I had deplored even as a boy in Tarsus, ran wild, screaming and laughing in a drunken frenzy of filth and debauchery.

Suddenly possessed of an uncontrollable rage, which has since many times given rise to much speculation with me, I broke from my companions and dashed through the portal and into the midst of the revelers who were gathered about an enormous statue on a marble block pedestal, the object of their idolatry.

"Stop!" I shouted. "The judgment of God is upon you!"

Unable to control my overpowering revulsion, I began lashing out at the pagans with my staff. Both male and female went down before the fury of my onslaught.

For a moment, struck sober by the sudden, violent interruption of their base activities, they stood in a circle around me.

Then, several of the men leaped forward and wrenched the staff from my hands and dragged me to a pillar by the door through which I had entered. There, to the accompaniment of wild laughter, I was bound and beaten to unconsciousness with my own staff.

Left prostrate and senseless by the pagans, who returned to their revelry, I was cut down and removed from the pillar by my companions, and then taken to a grove of trees by the sea, where my stripes were washed with salt water for healing. My first vague remembrances thereafter were the words of John Mark as to his doubts about continuing farther into the domain of the heathen, for Paphos was the seat of Roman authority and known to be given to all things godless.

Barnabas did not reply, probably himself possessed of doubts, but lifted my head and put beneath it his pack.

My first full consciousness brought pain the like of which I had never before experienced. My back burned as though it had been branded and my bones ached exceedingly. I was weak from the loss of blood, and at the first moan I uttered Barnabas lifted my head and gave me water. He wet a cloth and put it across the back of my neck.

"God forgive me," I said later, when I had the strength to speak. "Did I kill any of them?"

"I think not," said Barnabas. "And I believe they are too drunken to feel pain. But what can we do for you? You must be in torment."

I could not reply.

"We must move as soon as he is able," said John Mark. "The pagans may look for him."

As those words were said I fainted again, for the next I knew I was stretched on my stomach on a clean bed in a half-darkened room. How long I had lain so I did not know, but I was alone in a small chamber furnished with only a bare table, a chair, and the bed on which I lay. My back still ached, and my head throbbed mercilessly. The only light came from above, through an irregularly made window, and the light was the faint glow of a sunrise or a sunset; I knew not which. There were voices from somewhere in the house, and I must have made a noise on awakening, for Barnabas and John Mark were almost immediately through my door and beside me.

"Are you all right?" asked the big man.

"My . . . head is worse than my back."

"He needs nourishment," said the voice of an old woman who emerged from behind the massive frame of my friend as she spoke.

"Saul, do you think you can stand the touch of my fingers on your back?" asked John Mark, holding out a small bottle. "I have some oil which the old woman says will help the wounds."

I indicated that it would be all right. "Where are we?" I asked.

"At the house of a farmer, Malar, and his wife. They witnessed the beating, then came for you with an oxcart. You have been asleep all afternoon."

Mark's fingers hurt my back. "It . . . is . . . is it dusk, then?"

"Yes, we are in the hills west of the temple."

"Did I kill any of those people?" I winced again at the touch.

Barnabas delayed. "I think not. Malar tells us they come from the city of Paphos at intervals and consume such quantities of wine and a drug that they are insensible to pain."

"They are truly inhuman," said Mark.

"God forgive them," said Barnabas.

"This Malar and his wife," I said, "what do they know of . . . our mission?"

"John Mark and I have spoken to them of Christ, but they have some difficulty comprehending our meaning."

"Very simple people," said the young man.

"Thank God for them," I said.

At that moment the old woman, this time accompanied by her husband, came into the room carrying a wooden bowl with a wooden spoon in it.

"Saul . . . Malar and his wife," said Barnabas by way of introduction.

I looked up. "We are very grateful," I said.

The old people smiled. The man was very tall and strongly built for one of his age. He was beardless, and his deeply burned skin

89

was lined with furrows. The woman was short but stout, and both wore clean but simple garments of homespun.

"Can you rise to one elbow?" the woman asked.

With the help of John Mark I did, and Malar's wife gently fed me the bowl of broth which was made of a seafood.

"The beasts," said Malar.

There was hurt in Barnabas' face.

"Animals," said the old woman. "Nothing but animals dressed in human form."

"Do not judge them," I said. "I deserved what I got."

The old woman paused, the spoon halfway to my mouth, looking inquisitively into my eyes.

"They have not heard the truth of Jesus Christ," I said. "Do not judge them."

The old woman fed me the broth, but continued looking inquisitively at me. "They know right from wrong," she said.

For five days thereafter we stayed at the house of Malar. During the hours of work, Barnabas and John Mark helped the old people in their fields, and I sat in prayer and meditation beneath the branches of a big tree, feeling the gentle breeze from the sea which lay visible to the south.

One night we sat together in the house and talked of Jesus Christ, the old people listening intently and seeking to grasp the significance of our message.

Malar, his leathery face half illuminated in the dim light of the lamp on the table beside him, said, "But my wife and I live peaceably here. We work for our bread and offend no man. We do what good we are able to do and love our neighbors. We are happy. What need have we to worship your God or your Jesus Christ, of whom, had we not helped you, we would never have known?"

"But my friends," I said, "it is precisely because you did help me that I am able to speak to you now of the greatest of all gifts, eternal salvation. Don't you see that God has decreed it so? He reveals himself in strange and glorious ways and thus gives men the opportunity for eternal life with him."

"But you indicate that the alternative is damnation. What of my neighbor Phineta? He is a good man who did not take you in because he did not—and does not—know of your trouble, nor of you existence. Is he damned?"

"Your neighbor is the responsibility of those like yourself who have heard the gospel. I repeat—God speaks when and where he will, and after that the responsibility is with man to accept or reject. Damnation results from the rejection of revealed truth."

And so it went until the day we took our leave of the old people. What went on within their souls, I, of course, had no way of knowing, but I have prayed many times since that they might somehow have accepted the Lord and preached him in the regions thereabout.

But those were, nevertheless, happy days, and it was with some heaviness of heart that we departed the little place. John Mark, in particular, had developed a fondness for the old people, particularly the woman, and he walked for some miles in silence after we left them.

A day later we paused at a tiny cove just outside the great city of Paphos whose glistening structures were visible to the northwest.

"This," said Barnabas as we looked down upon the creamy foam, "is said to be the very spot where Aphrodite rose from the sea."

It was not difficult to imagine how the legend had originated at this place. The water was the deepest blue, and where it lashed against the stark white rocks the bubbles were like diamonds in sunlight.

"How could they so distort God's beauty?" said John Mark.

The young man's question went unanswered as we stood entranced with the beauty. I saw in the water in one flashing moment the vague form of an exquisite face which I bade leave my mind with words of the duty God had set for us.

"Well, my good friends, shall we challenge the great city of Paphos for the Lord?" I smiled and put my arm across the shoulder of John Mark, and we went back down to the road.

Paphos, we found shortly, to be much the same as Salamis, only larger and policed by a garrison of Roman soldiers whose polished metal could be seen on every street. There was not here the aura of happy freedom we had encountered elsewhere on the island. There

91

were fewer smiles, and the people did not receive us so eagerly, being more concerned, it seemed, with their own pursuits and having little time for anything else. Our presence in the synagogues in the weeks that followed was met with something less than cordiality, and disputations became at times so heated that I was put to mind of the worst excesses of my lamented period in Jerusalem.

In the passage of time, we found ourselves occupying a position of some notoriety in the city. We were as much the object of curiosity as anything else, for Christianity as a force in that part of the world was practically non-existent. Those converts among whom we moved seemed to exist under a cloud of fear both of the Romans and of the pagan idolaters. They recoiled in horror at the retelling of my action at the temple of Aphrodite and seemed to wonder why I was not killed on the spot. The Aphrodite pagans would stop at nothing except an act of rebellion against the authority of Rome. I supposed they had spared me because to have murdered would have been to have put themselves at odds with the Roman courts, which, I can attest, can be swift in the punishment of offenders.

At any rate, we were—not unexpectedly—summoned within a month of our arrival into the presence of one Sergius Paulus, Roman proconsul in Cyprus, and who was many years thereafter to play a vital part in these events.

There was never more than the slightest doubt with us that the man had ought but a momentary diversion in mind, for his reputation was that he was a just man and one possessed of a noble, if at times unpredictable, nature. What we expected was that he would order a sort of command performance of psalm-singing and preaching, the like of which had undoubtedly been reported to him on the day of our first appearance in a Paphos synagogue. What we found was something else again.

The room into which we were ushered was large and colonnaded, with polished tile floor, and an elevated stage at one end. On this stage, in an ornately carved golden chair which was more a throne, sat Sergius Paulus, a handsome man under forty, flanked by two guards in uniform and two other men, one of whom was dressed richly as an advisor or chamberlain, and the other attired in a costume of almost ridiculous proportions.

Had not the occasion been a solemn one, this strange man might have given us all call to laugh, for he was robed with a black, glossy material over whose surface had been sewn various sized Stars of David in scattered abundance. On his head he wore a tall, peaked hat, black and also covered with stars, and in his hand he held a black, gold-knobbed stick which he brandished, on our approach, like a wand of magic. His beard was black and hung to his waist, and his eyes blazed like the eyes of a madman.

"Stop and bow," commanded the man I assumed to be a chamberlain.

We stopped but we did not bow.

"You will bow to the proconsul," demanded the man.

Perhaps perceiving the determination of our uncompromising faith, the proconsul waved his deputy to abstain from the formality, and he leaned forward, his elbow on the arm of the chair.

"I bid you greeting, sirs," he smiled, "and trust you have not been inconvenienced by my intrusion on your schedule."

The warmth of his greeting was unexpected. The deputy glanced with some disdain at his master and retreated another step, scowling then at us as did the strange one.

"We are not inconvenienced, sir," I said.

"Good," he said, and he leaned back again in his splendid chair. "Word of your . . . ministry . . . in the synagogues of the Jews has reached us."

He paused and glanced half amusedly from one to the other of his somber attendants, "and caused some . . . ah . . . debate hereabout . . . especially concerning the alleged working of miracles."

"All things are possible with the most high God," said Barnabas.

"And that," said the proconsul, pointing a finger at my bold friend, "that is another thing. You speak of one God."

"That we do, sir," replied Barnabas. "We speak of the one true God and father of our Saviour, Jesus Christ."

"Do not listen," admonished the strange one in a sharp, disturbing voice, again brandishing his wand.

93

But as if not hearing, Sergius Paulus leaned forward. "Saviour from what?"

"From your sins," said Barnabas.

"Watch your tongue," said the deputy.

"Hear them out," said the proconsul. "My sins?"

"We have all sinned and stand convicted and unjustified before God, without Jesus Christ," I said.

The proconsul bowed his head. "This . . . Jesus Christ . . . was he not the carpenter's son who was crucified?"

"And arose," said Barnabas.

The deputy breathed a cynical laugh, and the face of the strange one became even more grim.

The proconsul paid no notice, and continued. "Arose from the dead?"

"To be seen again by many," said Barnabas.

"And where is he now?"

"In heaven . . . At the right hand of the most high God, his father," affirmed the big man.

The eyes of Sergius Paulus looked closely at each of us. "The young man . . . Is he also a believer? He does not seem to display any courage of conviction."

Barnabas stepped forward. "He is my nephew, sir, and he . . ."

"Let him speak for himself," said the proconsul.

"I believe in the power of Jesus Christ unto salvation," said John Mark.

"Well said, like a schoolboy rehearsed," said the proconsul. "What say you, Elymas? Well said, eh?" He had turned to the strange one as if in good-humored anticipation of a foreknown reply.

"Sheer folly," spat the man in black. "Let them display the power of their Jesus Christ by some manifestation."

The proconsul looked back to us and knew again that we were not to be compromised. He thought for a moment, then said "Perhaps they should first see something of your own power." Then he waited, not looking at his sorcerer until the latter, after some sinister mental workings, strode off and retrieved from behind one of the columns a sort of urn, smoking and supported by a metal stand almost as tall as himself. He set the object between the Roman and the three of us, then stood to the side, lifted his arms and uttered a chant of strange words, waving the wand above the urn. Suddenly a cloud of green smoke erupted in a billow from the urn; there was a pungent odor, and a voice, as from the smoke, said, "Hear not the words of the conspirators."

We stood for a moment transfixed by the evil exhibition, perplexed, as would have been any who had never before witnessed the like. The proconsul, seemingly pleased with the display, waited for further response.

Suddenly I was again seized with an excess of confidence, an unrestrainable exhilaration, unexampled except in my experience at the temple of Aphrodite.

I leaped forward, casting aside the urn and stand and seizing the wand from the hand of the magician. Taking the wand in both hands I cracked it in two across my leg and spilled out from a hollow recess in it a quantity of powder being active when mixed with another smoking substance, spilled now from the urn across the floor. Then I gazed into the eyes of the sorcerer and said, "O full of all subtlety and all mischief, you child of the devil, you enemy of all righteousness, will you not cease to pervert the right ways of the Lord?"

He retreated, stumbling against one of the columns.

I said "And now, behold, the hand of the Lord is upon you, and you shall be blind, not seeing the sun for a time."

The man then grasped at his eyes and fell to the floor crying "I am blind! I am blind!"

Sergius Paulus came forward and said "I believe. What would you have me to do?"

I laid my hand on him and said "Repent of your sins and serve the Lord."

And that day we baptized him and received him into the church of Jesus Christ.

The conversion of Sergius Paulus revealed the power of God in the city of Paphos. Jew and Gentile, hearing of the unprecedented event, flocked to our presence to hear the word of God. In time, a mighty church was established and organized with strength so that it might prosper unaffected by our leaving, which was imminently decreed by the Holy Spirit. We bade farewell to the procurator and sailed to Attalia, the seaport of the city of Perga, on the southern coast of Asia.

"Our course," I said to my companions the night of our arrival, "will be through Perga and into the interior of Asia."

Neither man replied immediately, their expressions unenthusiastic.

John Mark glanced at his uncle, and the big man looked at the floor.

"Is something the matter?" I asked.

John Mark's eyes dropped, and Barnabas arose and walked to the small window of our room. He looked out into the darkness, then turned back to me. "The Lord speaks and we obey, Paul (for such did I call myself after the conversion of Sergius Paulus), but you are, perhaps, not so aware as Mark and I of the dangers involved in the course you propose."

"I am aware," I said.

"The land is largely uncivilized," said John Mark. "The mountain travel is extremely perilous; there are thieves and cutthroats whom even the Romans have not been able to apprehend."

"I am well aware of the dangers in the Taurus Mountains," I said. "There are narrow passes along sheer cliffs, and torrents which would have to be forded. It won't be easy."

"What Mark is saying, I think," said Barnabas, "is that it might be advisable to ask the authorities for guides."

"Or for guards?" I said. "No—"

"What I am saying," interrupted John Mark, "is that I do not believe the Lord expects us to run headlong into foreseen dangers. It is one thing to encounter unexpected trouble but another to act as though trouble does not exist."

"You cannot avoid peril, Mark," I said. "We have at no time been promised an easy life in the service of Christ."

"The difference is between sense and foolhardiness," said the young man, his face flushed. "The route you propose would take us through territory populated by savages and rife with every peril a traveler could encounter. We will be of no service to Christ at the bottom of a chasm."

"You may go or stay," I said. "There is nothing compulsory in this, but the Lord has spoken, and I leave within the week."

Barnabas walked to a position between us. "Now let us not allow ourselves to fall into a personal dispute—not after all we have been through together." He looked from one to the other of us. "Perhaps we should sleep on this. It has been a trying day."

"I will feel no differently tomorrow," said John Mark, arising.

"Then you are of no further service on this mission," I said.

He turned quickly. "Does Barnabas have nothing to say about that? As I recall, he began this journey as leader."

"There is no leader but God," said Barnabas softly. "Now let us not—"

"Let him speak," I said.

Mark said nothing.

Barnabas went and stood beside him. "Where would you have us to go from here?" he asked.

"To Greece . . . Rome . . . There are millions of civilized peopl who have not heard of Christ."

"The time will come for Greece and Rome," I said, "but it is nc now."

"Then you go without me," said the young man, his voice trem bling.

"So be it," I said. "A man who is not ready to face death fc Christ has no business on this mission."

"Death?" The young man's eyes flashed. "Death? No, I a¡ not ready to die. I am ready to live. You have no monopoly o Jesus Christ. You do not love him one bit more than I do, eve though you seem to think he is yours exclusively."

"Now, Mark—" began Barnabas.

"What about you, Uncle," said the young man. "Where do yo stand in this?"

Barnabas looked straight into the eyes of his nephew. "If Go has spoken to Paul, then we must obey. God is the leader of th mission. There is no other. We must go into Asia."

"Then, goodbye," said John Mark, and he turned and left tl room. He sailed the following day from Perga toward Jerusalen

Whatever effects Mark's leaving and my involvement in it may have had on Barnabas were kept well hidden by the man as we set forth on the long inland journey which was to take us deep into the heart of Asia.

Barnabas was a man of deep passions and complete integrity who never, to my knowledge, engaged in personalities, choosing always to direct his mental and physical energies toward the one goal to which he had dedicated his life. He never once complained of any hardship, though I knew the inner conflicts concerning Rachel—and now John Mark—burdened him exceedingly. There had been no word of the girl at any place in Cyprus, and he had not mentioned her for months, so I knew that he must have finally resigned himself to the fact of her permanent loss. Now, when I had again been involved in a turn of events which hurt the man, I wanted more than ever to lay bare my soul to him, to take what blame I might deserve, but the words would not come when the times presented themselves.

I lay awake nights on the road, thinking of the girl. My guilt in respect to her dug deeply into my heart, and yet I could never rightly discern the source of my guilt. I had been justified in her case as in that of John Mark. I could not have taken her with me to Tarsus. There were no words I could have said to her, or to John Mark, except the complete truth, which had been precisely what I had done. How, I thought, is it possible to assume blame for engaging in the Lord's whole truth? And yet there has not, since that night in Jerusalem to this moment, been a waking hour when I have not been aware of this burden. It is always there even when I feel that God has forgiven me for all else I have done to my fellowman. It is the thorn of my affliction, the thing I have borne that the perfection of Christ might be magnified and that my service for him might be tenfold that of a man content.

So these thoughts, then as now, crept repeatedly through my mind as we picked and fought our way through the rock-bound wilds of Asia. No preconceived estimation of the tribulations we would encounter in this wasteland proved exaggerated. The rugged Taurus Mountains, snow-capped and boulder-strewn, wall the semi-arid plateau whose uncharted reaches were scattered about with the rude and uncouth populace we sought to reach with the truth of Christ. Threading narrow mountain passes, where a misplaced foot could have sent us plummeting into rampaging torrents far below, I more than once looked up to see a solitary figure framed against the sky waiting to descend with his band of robbers on more prosperous travelers. Our poverty, I am certain, served the blessed purpose of saving our lives on each such occasion. And the powerful grasp of my friend twice pulled me from the clutch of death in high wind which caught us scaling the sheer side of a cliff.

Days became weeks before we traded the perilous heights of the Taurus for the trackless deserts of Pisidia. Our difficulties were compounded by a variety of dialects, so that we were often forced to make our wishes known to the rough natives that we encountered by hand signs and drawing on the earth. When I could do so, I earned my food and lodging with the tentmakers, and Barnabas put his back to whatever task of labor he might find. Little of the land was arable, and he was often without hire, forcing us to share the meager wages I was blessed to be able to earn. God never left us hungered nor without at least a cave or mountain recess to protect us from the elements.

Our first major stop was the formidable city of Antioch-in-Pisidia. It was, as you might suspect, a most welcome sight to a pair of lonely wanderers and especially to the one whose happiest moments were spent among the thousands. We established ourselves with work and lodging, and on the Sabbath we went to a synagogue of the Jews which was the first we had entered in many weeks.

Now after the reading of the Law and the Prophets, the presiding elder, seeing that we were strangers, asked if we had words for the assemblage, and I stood. Beginning with the text we had covered that morning, I proceeded in faith to repeat the great sermon of the blessed Stephen as closely as I could remember, watching closely, as I did, the faces of the Jews. I addressed them in the manner of the rabbi, bringing forth the logic of Christ as fulfilment of the prophets, and as I spoke I held their rapt attention. There was no stirring or leaving in the course of it, and when I had finished, there were no disputations. At the time, I was not certain whether they were awed by the boldness of the new doctrine or held attentive by the sheer force of God's inspired truth, but they did not rise and threaten or revile or in any way challenge us, and when the message was complete we walked out through the midst of them.

On the sabbath following the synagogue was thronged by Jew and Gentile alike, there being many standing along the walls and outside the building. Seeing such a mixed gathering, I determined that, God willing, and the elders willing, I would that day center the message I might be privileged to deliver on the theme of Jesus Christ as Saviour of all men—of whatever race or creed—who might call upon his holy name. God willed, and I spoke. The result was great consternation among the Jews. I could see it mounting as I delivered the address, and when I had finished, one of the Jews rose and blasphemed the name of Jesus. "An imposter and a fraud!" he exclaimed. He had been in Jerusalem during the time of this carpenter's son. "The Galilean brought no triumph over the conquerors of Israel, but was nailed to a cross between two common criminals!" And another Jew arose. "What is your authority for entering the synagogue of God and preaching salvation to the heathen?"

"Yes! Yes! By what authority do you promise God's blessing on the heathen?" cried more of the Jews arising and gesturing toward us with clenched fists. Then there were others, and the voices became louder and the gestures more violent, so that I knew we must leave before the advent of a riot.

The Jews were motivated by envy that the hearts of the Gentiles had been touched. So I turned my back upon the Jews and bade the Gentiles follow us to a place outside the city, saying to the Jews, "It was necessary that the word of God should first have been spoken unto you, but seeing you reject it and judge yourselves unworthy of everlasting life, we turn to the Gentiles, for thus was it decreed by God."

Many Gentiles were that day saved, being baptized in a river which flowed nearby. The message of salvation we brought was published throughout the region, and we were received with joy and gladness among the Gentiles.

But the Jews stirred up the leaders of the people against us and sent a committee to seek us out and expel us from the city. We were forced to gather our belongings quickly at a late hour and were cast out from the city in the darkness of night.

Shaking the dust off our feet against the persecutors at Antioch we took three days' journey east to Iconium, achieving there
much success among both Jew and Greek who gathered in the synagogue to hear the good news of salvation for all men. Many were
added to the church before the Jews incited the Gentiles against us,
plotting subtly to lay hands on us and to stone us. But we got
word of the plot and departed secretly, turning south toward Lystra
and arriving in that city within a day. At Lystra, we followed our
procedure of securing work and devoting the Sabbaths and other
free hours to spreading the gospel.

One afternoon, shortly after leaving work, we stood in the midst
of a large gathering in the marketplace. There were both Jews and
Gentiles, men and women, dressed in rags and in finery; and they
gave close attention to our words, especially a severely crippled man
who cried out to be brought close so that he might see and hear.
His legs were twisted grotesquely beneath his body, and his back
was bent into a bow, and when he was carried in close by two of
the poor, the sight of him stirred my heart, and I admired the depth
of his desire to attend to the word. The Holy Spirit again descended
upon me, and when I felt his force and warmth I cried out in a
loud voice: "Stand up on your feet!"

All eyes turned from me toward the cripple, and he immediately leaped to his feet and walked, clapping his hands and crying out with joy at the wonder which had been worked in him. He ran from one to the other of them in the street exclaiming "Look! I can walk! I can stand and walk!"

They fell back in amazement, speechless and wide-eyed with wonder at the miracle they had beheld. When we departed their midst, some followed to our inn and stood outside our door throughout the night.

The following morning, on leaving for our work, we were swept up in a great press of humanity. Some bowed or prostrated themselves before us, reverently intoning the words "Jupiter" and "Mercury," as others, like escorts, guided us to a prearranged place of assembly near a gate of the city. There they had staked out oxen and gathered garlands and were as if in preparation for some pagan rite, for men in strange costume stood on either side of an altar on which were placed a ceremonial knife and various containers enigmatically inscribed.

We were ushered to the forefront, and the two men like priests bowed. "Hail! Jupiter! Hail! Mercury! Come down from Mount Olympus to dwell in our midst! All hail!"

The crowd fell to their knees and extended their arms and raised and lowered their upper bodies in unison, chanting a strange intonation of praise and reverent fear.

Barnabas, perceiving their intent, ran among them and began lifting them to their feet crying: "Men and brothers, do not do this thing! We are but men as yourselves. Get up! Get up! This is blasphemy!"

I ran in front of the altar and in a loud voice admonished all assembled to rise and return to their homes and to their work, explaining our purpose for being in their city. Then Barnabas, when the people did not understand, rent his clothing in his vexation and revealed his flesh, that it was the same flesh as theirs and in no wise godly or glorious. And I did likewise, taking one of the knives and cutting the flesh of my arm so that it bled. I walked among them showing the blood and imploring them to cease from such un-

104

speakable vanity both now and forever and to beg forgiveness of the one true God whose son we had come to glorify.

After much pleading they dispersed, but not all were persuaded by our demonstration, an apparent fact which gave us much cause for concern lest ever again our work appear to bring glory to ourselves. We spent the day in disturbed contemplation, and that night ate little, but sat in silence on either side of a small table in the center of our room. We had no light but the pale flicker of a candle, and the hovering gloom was a suitable environment for the dejected state of our spirits. Looking up from my empty plate at the massive, wavering shadow of my friend cast upon the bare clay wall behind him, I was brought to understand how the misguided could have mistaken him for the father of the gods.

"Do you think, Paul," said he, "that God was testing us?"

"I do not know, but it was certainly the most disturbing thing that has happened."

"It means," said my friend, arising, "that we must assure that it does not happen again. These people are unlike any that we have met, and—"

At that moment, the sound of many footsteps came from outside our door. I quickly arose and stood tense as the door was suddenly thrust open revealing at least ten men, some of whose faces were familiar and whom my mind fought to identify. One, in the forefront, a tall, thin man with twin-spiked beard, spoke.

"You are the men called Paul and Barnabas?" It was more accusation than question, spat out in hatred.

"What is the meaning of this?" asked Barnabas.

"We have no interest in you," the man said. "It is the small one who has blasphemed the God of Israel."

At that moment it came to me where I had seen the man. He had been the first to stand and curse the name of Jesus Christ on our second sabbath in the Pisidian Antioch. His attack had been so vile that his face had been etched deeply on my mind. And some of them with him were of those we had rebuked for worshiping us that morning.

"Yes, he is the one," said a man in the background.

"Take him," said another. And the three or four in the forefront came toward me.

Barnabas quickly stepped between the mob and myself, and with his great strength pushed them back so that some fell into others in a heap on the floor. There was cursing and a scrambling of knees and elbows, and I stepped forward and took my friend by the arm. "I will go with them," I said.

"But Paul—"

"It is better," I said. I took my friend's hand and smiled, not knowing whether this would be the last that I would see of him. "God be with you," I said.

"I am going with you," he said.

"No," said one of the Jews who had picked himself up from the floor. "We want only the man Paul, for transgressing the law. You, big bull, get out of town if you value your life."

With that they laid hands on me and took me out of the inn and through the streets to a building some blocks away which served as their prison. There I was thrown into a small, filthy room and locked behind a heavy door. There was no light and only a small window high in the wall opposite the door. I was not fed that night nor contacted in any wise but spent the darkness hours squatting on the slimy floor amid the ordure and decay, praying constantly that the will of the Lord might prevail.

Within an hour after the first dim light seeped through the slit of window, iron bars clanked and my door was pulled open. The man with the spiked beard came past the jailer and stood framed in the doorway. With one hand he covered his nose and with the other he pointed a bony finger at me. "You have been judged guilty of transgressing the Jewish law and are sentenced to be taken from this place to the Eastern Gate and stoned until you are dead. Take the prisoner!"

At his command, and as my knees were wont to buckle under me, they took me into the midst of them, some spitting upon me and others kicking and pummeling me with their fists. I was dragged through the streets, the crowd growing in size and in the bitterness of their feeling. Blows fell about my head and shoulders rendering me near senseless, and my arms were all but pulled from their sockets as I was dragged toward the place of stoning. Twice I lost consciousness, fell and was picked up and pulled by my hair, my legs and arms scraping, bloody and raw, across the cobblestones.

When the wall was reached I was spun around and thrown violently against it so that I fell to my hands and knees. Then the first stone tore into my shoulder, and I fell flat. The missile hit my bone with such force that a gash was opened and blood gushed from the blue mound. Another stone struck the top of my head, then another . . . I was sick, then weak . . . and the blackness closed in about me . . .

In the world to which the cast stones consigned me I stood on a certain level of a mountain on which weaving, moaning thousands perched precariously at various pockets and crevices above me. Their haunting cries were directed down to where I stood, I being somehow empowered to rescue them and take them to their common goal, which was the summit. Below lay a fearsome, fog-shrouded, bottomless pit which at intervals claimed those grown too tired to hold on—or who gave up hoping for rescue. Their screams, as they fell, tormented my soul and compounded my guilt, and as each fell directly past me the face on the doomed body became the face of Rachel. So agonizing was the spectacle that I could not proceed, but sought to cover my own face instead. Hundreds fell, but the number on the precipice was not diminished, and there was about the whole vision an aura of hopeless frustration. I was totally responsible, and yet pitifully incapable of doing anything.

Then, as I fought and strained to the limit of my strength, voices echoed in the chambers of my mind and a dim haze of light displaced the nightmare. The broad, smiling face of my friend looked down upon me and his voice, as from some great distance, said "The Lord has spared him." Through the blur of my vision three more faces appeared whose features were not discernible.

"Praise God," said the voice of a woman.

"He has great strength," said the voice of a young man.

"He is the strongest man I have ever known," said Barnabas.

"Bathe his forehead, Eunice," said the voice of a woman.

107

"I need cool water, Mother," said another woman.

"I will go to the spring," said the young man.

Each last word spoken raced away, echoing to infinity, and I slowly began to be aware of the throbbing pain in every bone of my body. I cried out at a piercing stab in my right temple.

"My friend—Paul, what can I do?" said Barnabas. "Our Heavenly Father, spare thy servant we pray."

"The fiends have broken his skull," said a woman.

Barnabas spoke again, but the words dissolved into the blackness which again overtook me. When I awoke the second time night had fallen and I lay for a time trying to collect my thoughts and relate myself in time and place. The bridge to reality was the pain of my body, and I must have moaned, for again the face of my friend, illuminated in the light of a candle, appeared above me.

"Barnabas . . . ?"

"Yes, my brother. Are you any better?"

"The pain . . ."

"Yes, yes I know, but you shall recover. We have been in prayer these hours and the Lord has spoken. You are spared for his purpose."

I held the big hand tightly.

"Your strength is as great as ever," he said, a trace of happiness in his voice.

"Where . . . Where are we?"

"At the home of a woman of God named Eunice, whose mother, Lois, and son, Timothy, have not ceased to wait upon us since the stoning."

"You brought me here?"

"With the help of the boy, Timothy. When the Jews had left you for dead outside the gate, I came to claim your body and had discovered a spark of life when the saints of God came to me and offered the hospitality of this house."

"God's grace is boundless."

"He does not forsake us, Paul."

I tried to raise myself, but fell back.

"Do not move," said Barnabas. "You must remain still."

"But . . . Are we not a liability to these people? If the Jews should return and—"

"We will leave when you are able."

"Soon . . ."

"When you are able, my brother. Now, you must rest. I will put the candle on the table and make my bed across the room, so if you need me I will be nearby."

"My good friend."

"I will be here if you need me."

So I slept, and in the five days that followed I regained my strength through the power of God and the ministration of Barnabas and the good people of that home. Christ had come into their lives during our first gospel service at Lystra, for the women had been in the marketplace and had heard and accepted the truth and then told the boy.

Timothy spent hours with me, his eager young mind grasping for more and more of the story of Jesus Christ and his promise to the world. My head swathed in cloth and my body bathed in healing oil beneath my robe, I sat propped up in bed and discoursed with the boy, learning from him of the manners and customs of his people as he learned of the Lord from me. He was much in appearance like John Mark, though at fifteen somewhat younger. His alert dark eyes displayed the same bright enthusiasm I had seen in Mark at first, and his lithe, angular frame the same youthful vigor. His questions were about what we had seen in our travels and what the sea was like and why we had come so far to tell the story of a man I had never seen. The boy's father, who had died in Timothy's first year, had been a Greek and his mother Eunice was a Jewess, and the races were well met in the boy. He seemed to embody the best characteristics of each—the inquisitive nature of the Greeks and the intellectual determination of the Jews, and I loved him for the bountiful measure of his heavenly Father which I saw in him. On the day of our leaving he came to me with tears in his eyes.

"Brother Paul," he said, "I would go with you if you would have me."

His mother came forward and put her hand on his arm.

"God bless you, my son," I said. "But what would your mother and your grandmother do with no man about the house?"

"The Lord needs men here in Lystra as he does on the road," said Barnabas.

"You have many years ahead of you," said the grandmother, Lois.

The boy thought for a moment, then said: "The great Alexander of Macedonia was barely older than I when he conquered the world."

"And he wept," said the old woman.

"Every man has his own world to conquer," I said.

The boy looked down, then up again. "Will you write?" he asked.

"We will write," I said.

"We must go, Paul," said Barnabas, who had been standing somewhat impatiently just outside the door keeping an eye out for any sign of the Jews.

I took the hands of each of the saints in turn. "Will we see you again?" asked Eunice.

"I pray so," I said. "And God's richest blessings on this house."

"You should not be traveling," said old Lois, a tear in her eye.

"I have the strongest right arm on earth to bear me up," I said, nodding toward Barnabas. "And this staff that Timothy has cut for me is fit for a king."

"Good-bye, Paul," said the boy.

"Good-bye, my boy," I said, and I turned quickly, so that he would not see my eyes, and took the arm of my friend. We went as inconspicuously as two men, one leaning on the other, could go, through streets not yet awakened, south toward the city of Derbe.

A week's clumsy journey found us entering that place whose population and culture were Greek and whose religion was the worship of pagan gods. We found at first, as the hand of God reached down to heal my body and restore my strength, little else encouraging; but as the days passed, the Lord blessed our endeavor, and many were added to his number. We were in no wise abused at Derbe, but made many friends and established a vital church of Gentiles under the leadership of the devoted Gaius. We learned in time that the legalist Jews who had instigated my stoning had set out after us from Lystra, but had turned back after a day's journey, thus enhancing the estimation, which shall ever be mine, of Derbe as a place of refuge from evil. The Lord always provides in some wise for his servants in any manner of adversity, enabling them to bear and giving them respite from their sufferings. My wounds healed in Derbe, in comparative calm and safety, and in this atmosphere, Barnabas and I made a momentous decision for the Lord.

Our direction from the Pisidian Antioch had been generally east and south toward our headquarters in Antioch of Syria and our hearts had often on this perilous journey longed for a return home to our friends. But after much prayer it was decided in Derbe that the purposes of the Lord would best be served if we retraced our steps and revisited our churches in Asia, reinforcing weaknesses which might have occurred among the brethren and reassuring where reassurance might be required. It would be a journey fraught with dangers even greater than those we had already encountered, but the thousands which we had reached and won were mere children in the faith, living in the midst of pagan idolatry and wavering on the brink of return to the ways of sin.

I praise the Lord for putting to us this additional charge, for the return journey, though long, was blessed with the Lord's safety and was the most rewarding Christian experience of my life. We were received with boundless love throughout the region of Galatia, and, as I wrote later to the saints, they received me as an angel of God, even as Christ Jesus. My prepossession with thoughts of Rachel and of the others must at times have sapped the spirit of my ministry; but the blessed children of God forgave the lapses, though they knew not the source, and overlooked my temptation. And I am convinced that they would not have hesitated to pluck out their own eyes and give them to me had I so desired. My love for the Galatians was, and is, boundless.

The retracing of our steps led us back finally to the port of Attalia where we embarked for home.

111

Our return to the midst of our brethren in the home church was an event to which no other word than "triumphant" could be ascribed. Barnabas and I were greeted with unabated enthusiasm and were called upon to recount time and again the fruits of our mission, thus gladdening the hearts of those zealous Christians at Antioch. The church in that city, we found, had continued to succeed no less completely than ourselves, and great numbers came to hear the message of salvation at each meeting. There was even a vital movement among the youth, with the new cause of Jesus Christ possessing eager minds as completely as it had those of their elders hungry for the good news of salvation. Antioch was a blessing to the Lord, and we gave ceaseless praise.

Not so, however, the church at Jerusalem. It soon fell to our ears that certain of the brethren from that city had come to Antioch teaching that circumcision is necessary to salvation. This creeping in of the anti-Christian legalistic Judaism disturbed us greatly, for not only did it cause perplexity and dissension among those babes in Christ in both churches, but it also revealed the lack of comprehension among those spreading the falsehood, of the truths of Christianity. Jesus Christ himself had said: "No man seweth a piece of new cloth on an old garment: else the new piece that filled it up taketh away from the old, and the rent is made worse. And no man putteth new wine into old bottles: else the new wine doth burst the bottles, and the wine is spilled, and the new bottles will be marred: but new wine must be put into new bottles."

These Jews professing Christianity still did not realize that belief in Jesus Christ as Saviour is sufficient to salvation. They did not realize that either Christ is all or he is nothing. To have other requirements than himself to salvation is as saying that he is not enough. It is to lessen, nay detract, from his complete and total godliness.

To these men I was a dangerous extremist. To them all non-Jews were unclean, and these legalists went about spreading their poison among the Christian saints. So great was this disruption in Jerusalem of the wonderful thing Christ had built through us that barely twenty years after its establishment the church was on the brink of a disastrous split.

But cool heads prevailed, and a series of conferences was arranged in Jerusalem for the purpose of finding a solution to this seemingly insurmountable obstacle to the program. Barnabas and I were sent to that city as representatives of the Antioch church and the Antioch philosophy. At Barnabas' suggestion we took with us a man named Titus, a Greek uncircumcised, whose Christian witness was dynamic and above reproach, our purpose being to demonstrate the power of Christ in the life of any man no matter what his race or inheritance of creed. After much deliberation in which the legalists first demanded that Titus be circumcised, then recanted in the face of our irrefutable, inspired oratory, the Council of Jerusalem decided in favor of Christ, and the church was saved. Letters were sent then to all the churches informing them of the decision, and I, especially, rejoiced in my heart at the significance of it all. For I myself had been once a Pharisee chain-bound by the legalistic yoke, and I knew what that condition could do to a man.

Thus reinforced in mind and spirit, the three of us returned to Antioch and set back to the task of spreading the gospel.

The winter of the fifty-first year after the birth of Christ was the most severe in my memory. The trade routes through the mountains around Antioch were blocked by snow, as were many roads on flat land outside the city. Ships were tied at anchor at the docks, and commercial life was at a standstill for many weeks at a stretch. I had attached myself to a tentmaker of the city and at that place during off hours had expounded the gospel, so that the building, a low-roofed shed, became a meeting place for all those hungry for news of salvation. Barnabas and I continued in positions of leadership in the Antioch church and enjoyed continued success in our individual tasks. The Lord, in preparation for great things ahead, added to our number the man Silas.

My first impression of Silas, who had come up to us from Jerusalem, was that he was bigger than he truly was. Perhaps this had to do with his spirit, or with the vigor which he exercised in accomplishing whatever he was given to do. But I liked him and immediately recognized in him a vital servant of Christ. There were times, indeed, when he brought to mind the picture I had formed of Jesus. His face was placid, his hair long and the color of wheat and his beard neatly kept. He was a man of engaging personality and one sought in any gathering of the brethren.

Now when the first warm breezes of spring began to drive winter's chill from our bodies and when life began to be restored to the city and to the land, the Lord laid it upon my spirit to set out again. It was as though a great burden had been lifted from my shoulders, as though a prison gate had been flung open, for trapped I was never meant to be. I went one morning to Barnabas before he had arisen and said: "Let us go again and visit our brethren in every city where we have preached the word of the Lord and see how they do."

The big man blinked, and when he had collected his thoughts, smiled and stretched. "Right now?"

"As soon as you can make arrangements."

He arose and went and poured water in a basin and splashed it on his face, then dabbed with a cloth.

"What do you say, my friend?" I asked.

"I shall have to quit my job," he said.

"The world is waiting, Barnabas. The world is waiting, and the Lord is waiting. There will be your job when you get back."

He looked at me, then laughed and put his hand on my shoulder. "I am ready, Paul," he said. "As a matter of fact I had been wondering when you would bound in here, smiling, and say what you just said."

"Then let us make arrangements to leave within the week."

He nodded. "I have another little surprise," he said, going to a corner and retrieving a letter from atop a little table. He held it up. "From John Mark," he said. "He wants to join us. He says that if we go again he wants to join us."

Every trace of gaiety left me. I turned.

"What is it, Paul?"

"We cannot take John Mark," I said.

"But why?"

"You know as well as I."

"Oh, Paul, you cannot be serious. You mean because he left us? But that was years ago. He was a boy then. He is a man now."

"I am sorry."

115

Barnabas hesitated, looking at me. He shook his head. "You have never forgiven him, have you? You have never forgiven him."

I walked across the room. "That really has nothing to do with it."

"No?"

"No. You know what we face out there. You know what it is like. We cannot again risk losing a third of our effort."

"He has begged our forgiveness, Paul. He is sorry . . . and he is a man now, a man who wants and needs to redeem himself."

"Men's souls are in the balance, Barnabas. We cannot be involved with men on whom we may not be able to count in an emergency. When I was injured, the mission was at a standstill because you had to take care of me. Men died without Christ because John Mark was not with us."

"Oh, come now, Paul."

"It is true, and you know it is true."

He looked at me, then lowered his head and paced a few steps and stopped. "Paul, do you think John Mark has prayed for forgiveness?"

"I suppose so."

"Then do you think God has forgiven him?"

"If he is truly repentant."

"But you do not forgive him?"

"It is not a matter of my forgiving or not forgiving—"

"I think it is. I think it is." He started pacing again, then stopped and pointed at me. "You know something, Paul," he said. "You are the foremost disciple of Christ—you are the greatest preacher in the world, but you lack one thing—you do not possess a spark of tolerance."

"That is unfair."

"Do you know what tolerance I mean? I am speaking of tolerance among your friends and brethren—not of the heathen, of your friends and brethren. You expect every man you know to live up to your own standards. Well, I will tell you something, Paul; they cannot do it. If they could, they would all be Paul, and you would not be the greatest preacher in the world."

His words cut me, and immediately they were released, he knew it. I could see it in his eyes. But he did not look away, nor did he indicate a softening.

"I do not," I said, "stand in judgment over any man. But I cannot take John Mark."

"Then you shall have to go without me, too," he said.

I looked at him and he at me, and there was no wavering. So I turned and left the room. I walked down the long street from the house of Barnabas, past the tentmaker's shed and into the midst of the city, not conscious of the sights or sounds of awakening. How long I walked I do not know, but I did not go to my work that day, and when it was dark I went to my room and prayed: "O God, have mercy on thy servant and let his judgments be not perverted by sentimentality. Keep thy servant strong in the way that is right and bless his paths. Let his ways be thy ways." I lay prostrate before the Most High that night and did not sleep.

On the following morning I went to the man Silas and took him with me before the elders of the church and, with his permission, asked that we be commissioned for a journey overland through Asia, the Lord having laid it upon my heart so to do. They granted the commission, and we left Antioch within the week, and I never saw Barnabas again.

Within the space of two weeks, we had rounded the bend where the great sea juts in between Antioch and the province of Cilicia and had entered the city of Tarsus. We found there that the little church I had organized during the eight years of my exile had thrived, and my old friends greeted us enthusiastically. Whatever feelings of guilt I had entertained concerning my abandonment of this assembly at the call of Barnabas were quickly erased, and we left shortly, encouraged by the attitude of the saints.

We attached ourselves to a long caravan making its way up through the Taurus mountains to the province of Lycaonia and its chief cities of Derbe, Lystra, and Iconium. As we moved slowly across the wastes of the kingdom of Antiochus, I spoke of many things to Silas and learned much in turn about him.

He was a man of considerable experience, having, since his youth, traveled in many lands and spent much time aboard ship as a crew member. He had been orphaned at an early age and had thus been forced to make his own way in numerous pursuits. He was a man who spoke with authority but without any vestige of immodesty, a self-educated man, wise in the ways of the world and thus highly qualified for the mission. But most interesting, he had met and talked with Jesus Christ in a marketplace of Jerusalem.

The Master had healed an old woman of a certain infirmity, and Silas, greatly impressed, had approached the Lord with a question which had been answered with a parable that had gone deep into the soul of my friend. He had gone then to his room and, after much thought and prayer, had accepted Christ as Saviour and dedicated his life to Christian service.

James, the Lord's brother, had sent him to Antioch, seeing his special talent and how it could be applied in the missionary endeavor. At times I must have worn thin his patience with my inquiries about the person of the Lord, but he always answered to the best of his memory. He had been one of hundreds driven into hiding during the time I visited persecution on the church, and he said that he had seen me twice on the streets of Jerusalem with my band of Temple guards. No more was said of that, as he perceived quickly the pain which any recollection inflicted upon me.

Now it had been my intention from the first to complete the effectiveness of our mission by the addition of a third member, and the boy, Timothy, a young man now, remained constantly in my mind. I disclosed the story of the lad to Silas and found him, through my description, almost as eager to arrive in Lystra as I.

"He sounds," said my friend, "like a young man I once knew aboard ship—eager, full of life, a ray of sunshine among a dismal crew."

"I hope the resemblance does not go that far," I laughed. And Silas, puzzled momentarily, then laughed with me.

When we did arrive in Lystra and had made our way to the home of Eunice, we were received as members of that family, taken to their bosom, and extended every comfort their meager situation could afford.

"But where is Barnabas?" inquired Timothy, a man now, his voice lower and his bearing more restrained.

"He . . . has been commissioned back to Cyprus," I said, and mentioned nothing further of him, so that by my silence they knew the subject was closed.

"Well, it is good to have Silas," said old Lois, and that was the spirit thenceforth during the time that we were there.

On the second day we had finished the evening meal when I broached the subject which had lain on my mind for those months. Being well aware of what the young man meant in the lives of both women, I had waited until a time when we could all sit down together to put the proposal before them. "In short," I summed it up, "I believe Timothy is called of the Lord, and I know that we can use him."

The women did not reply, but Timothy indicated that his desire to serve as a missionary had in no wise lessened in the years we had been apart. He was older now and able to make his own decisions; the women knew it and did not stand in his way.

"But he will always be a little boy to me," said Lois, putting her hand to her eye.

Eunice did not speak, but when her son had made his decision, she embraced him and gave her blessing to the great endeavor to which he there dedicated his life.

So we made our plans and instructed Timothy in the duties which would be his. They were to be the same duties invested in John Mark, and we sealed the investiture with a prayer for God's guidance in the successful accomplishment of those duties this time. In order to enhance the young man's appeal to the Jews we must encounter, he was circumcised before we left Lystra. I made it clear to him that this was in no wise requisite to his salvation, but that it could be a valuable thing in dealing with Jews while in no way jeopardizing his or our position with the Gentiles.

Three days following Timothy's circumcision we bade farewell to the women, whose tear-filled eyes bespoke the depth of their love for the young man. We proceeded north toward Iconium and the Pisidian Antioch, then back to Iconium, and north through the province of Galatia to Tavium and Ancyra. In those places which I had visited before, we gave comfort and assurance to the brethren, and in the others we established churches for the Lord.

The loneliest and longest single leg of journey that I ever attempted was the expedition west from the little city of Ancyra across the wilds of the north of Asia. Months of hunger and hardship were consumed in traversing this largely uncharted and sparsely pop-

120

ulated region, wherein were found no major cities and only occasional pagan villages to whose inhabitants we preached the gospel. At one time we thought to turn north into the province of Bithynia, but were divinely directed to continue on westward.

It was the fall of the year when we set foot in Troas, on the northwest coast of Asia. Footsore and exhausted in body and spirit, we decided to call Troas our pivotal westward point, and, after a time, to turn back south and east toward Jerusalem. In that manner we could encounter many cities we had not then visited as well as some which we had, and thereby extend the mission.

But this was not to be allowed of the Lord. Twice we made plans and were to the point of booking passage on ships when the Lord intervened and said that we were not yet to leave, and this perplexed and disappointed us for we were greatly desirous of returning to our loved ones.

While waiting for the divine will to be made known in this place, rich with a heritage of Homeric tales and battles, of Troy and the Trojan horse, we preached the truths of Jesus Christ to the sailors and fishermen and to all the people who would hear. Timothy had secured for us a small cabin near the banks of the Aegean, and though crude it suited our meager needs. Silas found work at the docks, and as neither Timothy nor I could find employment, we lived off the good man's earnings.

We had not been in Troas many days when I was seated, as was my custom in late afternoon, on the banks of the sea. The light of the sun lay crimson across the water, and my mind had long since turned to thoughts of the infinite power and wisdom and purpose of God. And there, near the place where Xerxes had reviewed three million Asiatics with whom he had hoped to bring the western world to his feet, I was in prayer that we might be included positively in that great panorama of events which is the divine will of God. My thoughts were miles away when the voice of Timothy came to me from behind. I turned to see him descending the little bank which rimmed my stretch of the beach.

"You have a visitor, Paul," he said. "A Christian and a physician from Philippi."

I arose. "His name?"

"Luke."

"Luke? I know no Luke."

"Well, he knows of you. He has come across the sea this day to see you."

When we arrived at our little cabin, Silas had come home from his work and was seated at our table across from the stranger. There was bread and wine on the table.

"Ah, Paul," said my friend, arising. "May I present Dr. Luke, a disciple of Jesus Christ from Macedonia."

The stranger arose and extended his hand. He was a tall, well-built, dark-haired man of about twenty-five, clean shaven and well-featured. He reminded me of James, the Lord's brother, in the regality of his bearing. He wore a rich brown robe and an emerald ring.

"We are honored," I said, taking his hand.

"I have looked forward to meeting you for some time," he said, and he spoke our tongue with the slightest accent and with the easy precision of the intellectual.

Timothy brought me our one other chair, then seated himself at my feet.

"May I pour you a glass of wine?" asked Silas of me.

I nodded. "And fill our guest's."

"And you, Timothy?" asked Silas.

"You will forgive me for intruding," said Luke, "but I come on a twofold mission of some importance."

"You are welcome here," I said.

He bowed, then leaned forward, his forearms on the table. "Have you decided on your itinerary from Troas?"

"We wait on the Lord," I said.

"Would you consider extending your mission to Macedonia?"

"If the Lord directs."

"Of course," said Luke, "but the situation is this—and not only in Macedonia—that there is a great need for Christian work among the women. They are abused, treated like cattle or worse by the men—especially the men of the pagan countries. Consider it and

122

you must see that their lot is one of misery and drudgery. They are as much enslaved as any Nubian chained to Roman oars, and our Christian ministry cannot be considered in any wise complete while this is the case."

"What you say is true," I said, "but we have never denied the word to women in any place."

"And that is precisely why I have come this distance to see you," said Luke. "You are especially the missionary to the Gentiles and unfettered by traditions which obstruct the freedom of the Gospel. I come to plead with you to bring your message to Macedonia, and particularly to the women of Macedonia."

Timothy looked up at me, then lowered his head.

"We had hoped to return home," I said. "But that does not seem to be the will of God. Silas?"

"You lead and I follow," said the good man. "I had thought that it would be good to return to Jerusalem, but this is the Lord's mission, and he may be speaking to us."

"Timothy?"

"I am with you, Paul," he said, and I put my hand on his shoulder. "Besides," he said, "I have never seen the land of the great Alexander."

Luke smiled, "You will pray about it then?"

"You may be assured of that," I said. "But you spoke of a twofold purpose."

Luke leaned back in his chair. "Yes," he said, "there is another reason, a personal one, a selfish one in fact. There is a woman of Philippi, one of many, who is afflicted with an ailment I cannot cure. It is an affliction of the mind and therefore, sadly, outside my realm of understanding."

"We are not physicians," said Silas.

"But you heal," said Luke.

"When the spirit of the Lord is upon us," I said.

"But if you came to Philippi you would consider her?"

"Of course," I said.

"Then I am happy," said the physician. "I can cope with the body, but the mind is another thing. I must tell you that this woman is being misused as a soothsayer by a devilish syndicate of unscrupulous men. They are playing upon the superstitions of the pepole and becoming wealthy and powerful."

"How is it, then, that you are involved with her?" asked Silas.

"That is the strange part of it," said Luke. "She is aware of the unnatural spirit which tortures her, but is unable to cope with it. She sought me out."

"And you could do nothing?" I said.

"Nothing whatever. Physically she is as sound as you or I."

"I have seen this before," I said. "It is as if Satan himself has gained a stranglehold on the mind and will not let it go."

"Do you think it is the result of sin in the person involved?" asked Timothy.

"I do not know," I said. "I do not believe that it is in all cases, though I have seen minds so degraded by choosing the things of the flesh that any power for good was destroyed."

"I have seen men who thought they were pursuing the things of God whose minds were in the same condition," said Silas.

"Of whom I was chief," I said.

"I did not mean . . ."

"Of course you did not, my friend," I said. "But it is a fact and one which I cannot change." I arose. "And now, our dear physician, it is time for us to leave for prayer meeting, and we would be highly honored if you would come and speak to the brethren, for I am certain they have grown weary of the sight of my face."

Three days later, the physician, Silas, Timothy, and I had crossed the north Aegean, landing at the port of Neapolis, and were approaching, by the great Egnation Highway, the thriving city of Philippi. The day after our meeting with Luke I had seen a vision of a man standing across the Aegean on the shores of Macedonia, beckoning and uttering these words: "Come over into Macedonia and help us." This was the sign from God for which we had been waiting, and, considering the presence of Luke, we took it as indicating an immediate departure.

Timothy's homesickness vanished as we set foot in Philippi, for this was known to him as the city which had been the fortress of Philip of Macedon and the base from which Philip's son, Alexander, had set out for the conquering of Asia and the Persian Empire. Now, it was the colony of Rome, but through the eyes of Timothy it was still supremely the dwelling place of the Great Alexander who had wept when he could find no more worlds to conquer. When the rest of us collapsed from weariness in the inn room which was Luke's home and office, Timothy was off filling his mind with the wonders of the city and of the land where Alexander had lived.

I digress now to savor those things which Macedonia conjures in my mind. When I say the word, I think of a people whose

125

spirit of unselfishness and nobility are without example among the children of God. I have tried to express something of this feeling in epistles to the Philippians and the Thessalonians. I love these people with all my heart and have nothing of them but love in return. When I think of them, I think of pride and courage perhaps remnant of the time when they ruled the world, and I think of benevolence which knew no bounds of time or distance.

I think of that great highway on which Philippi sits, and of the Roman legions tramping along its lava pavement bound for Asia— or bound home from Asia. I think of the soft blue of distant mountains across wide plains whereon mighty battles were fought. I think of white houses with white walls about them and of spreading elms and cypresses and mulberries. I think of poor farms worked hard by poor but liberal people made poorer by persecutions endured for the cause of Christ. And, symbolically, I think of a synagogue of Jews in Beroea who not only did not mistreat us, but accepted us as brothers and listened to all we had to say of the Lord.

We met Lydia on a sabbath. She had gathered the little band of women who worked for her, and they had assembled on the banks of the river Gangites to pray and to worship God, as had become their custom. All of them turned, surprised, as we came through the trees. I suppose if Luke had not been with us they might have run, and justifiably so, for we were rough and hard looking from the rigors of the life we had led for those many months. But Luke introduced us, and I may say now that this Lydia was the first truly beautiful woman I had seen in more years than I could recall.

She wore her purple in a fine garment which enhanced the beauty of her dark eyes. Her black hair glistened in the Macedonian sun, and her skin was smooth. I remember the smoothness of her skin because I knew she was no more than ten years younger than myself, but there were no wrinkles in her face, and her hands were smooth and soft. I spoke that morning the simple message of salvation, which is really the only message I have to speak, but I felt as though my words were clumsy, and I knew I was neglecting

126

the four or five others who were with her. I did not, could not, speak for long, but when I had finished she came forward with the others and was baptized in the waters of the Gangites.

And I think often of Helen.

I think of what the Lord did with her. Never was his power more clearly demonstrated. (Never except in my own case.) I remember that Luke had asked us to speak near an intersection of two streets in the marketplace at Philippi. This, he had said, would surely bring out the distressed woman in whose cause he had sought us out, for she plied her black arts in the area and did not miss a public gathering.

So we had bowed to Luke's request and had gathered a large crowd of the curious of every estate when, in the midst of our message, we were startled by a wild and piercing stream of chatter. Turning, we beheld in the middle of the street a creature, wild-eyed and of otherwise demented mien, unkempt of hair, but attired in expensive, if gaudy, raiment.

"These men," she screeched, "are the servants of the most high God, who show unto us the way of salvation."

Again and again she said the words.

Now Silas and I were amazed, for though she appeared insane, she spoke in truth. This was the first time such an occurrence had befallen us, and I was perplexed at the meaning of it. This was surely the woman in question (Luke could not be with us that day), but if she spoke in truth, wherein lay our duty to the Lord and to Luke? We were deeply puzzled, so we did nothing at the time, but went away determined to pray on the thing and to discuss it with the physician.

That night, seated in the large room of Lydia's house, we told Luke what had happened and, describing the damsel to him, found that she was truly the woman in question.

But Silas said, "Perhaps this strange circumstance is the will of God in this way: The woman, as Luke says, has a great following among the people because of her strange powers. The crowd we gathered today by the marketplace was not large, but if the merchants and people thereabout hear this woman, in whom they have faith, disclaiming in our favor, would she not be highly effective in the capacity of a herald?"

No one answered. Luke was, I knew, wrestling with the ethical aspects as I was with the spiritual.

"Is it possible," I asked of Luke, "that she fakes this clairvoyance for some reason? Perhaps she fears for her life if she is being enslaved."

"I do not think so," he said. "She may well fear for her life, but I do not believe she is mentally balanced."

"I agree with Luke," said Lydia. "I have seen this woman many times when selling my cloth near the marketplace. She has even accosted me on occasion, and I do not believe she is completely sane."

"Then how are we to account for the fact that she speaks the truth of Christ?" asked Timothy.

"I believe it is because she is truly clairvoyant," said our hostess.

"That is not possible," said the man of science.

"Then your explanation, doctor," I said.

Luke thought before answering. "The way I see it, she is mocking you. She . . . hears you speak, then simply, childishly, mocks your words—probably to the great humor of her masters. She is deeply disturbed. She needs help that I cannot give."

Lydia arose and crossed the room and stood near a window. Her hair blew in the gentle breeze off the plain. She turned. "Months ago," she said, "before I had met Luke or professed any faith in anything except myself and my business, I sustained a loss through theft of many rolls of cloth. I went to the authorities, but got no help from them, for they were not disposed to help a woman who was also a successful rival of men. So, at my wit's end, I went to this clairvoyant, and I swear to you that she not only told me where the cloth was to be found, but who had stolen it and by what means."

"And you got your cloth back?" asked Timothy.

"I did."

"Any comment, doctor?" asked Silas.

"Yes, as a matter of fact," he said. "I would be willing to wager that if the truth were known, the masters of the damsel engineered the theft in the first place."

"Then why would the damsel tell Lydia?" asked Timothy.

"Because she hates the men. I tell you she is sick, and she is persecuted, and she needs the hand of God."

"I do not say that she does not need God," Lydia said, "but I could tell you other things just as strange. Some of my women have visited her."

"Well," said Silas, arising, "I believe I shall sleep on the question. What about you, my boy?" he said to Timothy.

The young man had been thinking, but when Silas spoke he looked up and smiled and nodded to our friend. He got up and, with Silas, thanked our hostess for the meal she had prepared for us. The two of them left the room, but Luke remained seated, deep in his thoughts. The physician did not notice as Lydia and I stole away into the yard.

Something the lovely woman had said had puzzled me. One annoying fault of mine has always been curiosity. We strolled into the garden and did not speak for a time. There was a slight chill to the soft wind, but the sky was clear and the moon so bright that the elms cast shadows against the white walls around the yard. We stopped by a rear gate. Across the Roman highway and toward the mountains lay the wide valley of Philippi.

"Alexander marshaled his troops on that plain," she said.

"Not so loud," I said. "Timothy may not have left."

She laughed, and it was the first beautiful laughter I had heard in months.

"You love him, don't you?" she said.

"As much as it is possible to love a friend," I said. "He is the son I never had."

"You have never married?"

"No."

She remained silent.

"Have you lived here long?" I asked.

"Nineteen—no, twenty years."

"Alone?"

"No. I was married. We came here from Thyatira. My husband had learned to make the purple dye from the secretion of a shellfish, but so had others. So we came here."

"And he . . . ?"

"Died. The third year."

"I am sorry."

"It has been a long time."

She turned and looked back toward the garden.

"Lydia . . ."

"Yes?"

"A while ago, in the house, you said there was a time when you thought only of yourself and your business. You sounded bitter. Somehow I cannot think of you as ever being bitter. If this is none of my business, tell me, but . . ."

"But what did I mean?" She looked down, inhaled deeply, then took a few steps away. "I had a daughter, a beautiful girl who was my life. When my husband died, she was my life. I gave her all that was in my power to give—too much, really.

"She grew up with too much. She was not a wild girl, but she was full of life. She was eighteen, and in love, she thought, with a Roman officer, a handsome and dashing young officer who was also full of life—and full of daring.

"When she was with him she was as reckless and uninhibited as . . . as I suppose I might have been thirty years ago. I told her to quit seeing him, to stay away from him, for no good could come of any of it. There was an argument, and she left, and she was killed on that highway, in a chariot he was driving too fast."

Lydia came back to the gate and looked out along the highway. "So I became bitter, full of hate for Romans, for the world, for myself. That was what I meant in the house. It's not a pretty thing to remember."

"I am very sorry."

She turned and smiled. "It is over. Life goes on. I don't hate any more. There is a void in my life. Guilt I suppose keeps it there. The last words she heard from me were angry words. I suppose if there is any hate it is for myself. But I have learned to live with myself, without hating Romans or the world. Christ has done that for me—and Luke has done all a man can do. I went to a doctor and found Christ, and now I have met the apostle Paul. God is good."

I shook my head. "You put me in exalted company," I said. "I am afraid that if people knew the Paul who does not show, they would not be so inclined to put me where I do not belong."

"Oh? And how is that?"

"Another story."

"I have all night."

I could not speak the things that cried out for speaking and I stood dumb, gripping the gate until its ridges cut into my hands.

"You are not being fair," she said.

"No. I am not a fair man, not really. The fairest thing I can do is to tell you that."

She smiled. "All right, Paul."

For three days following, Silas and I trod the streets of Philippi, bringing the message of salvation to all who would hear, giving special attention to the women of the city. And each day as we made our way through the crowded thoroughfares we were followed by the strange damsel.

She never called out in a derogatory manner, but stayed with us continually, never ceasing her insane chatter. Silas had been correct in that the fact of her presence drew hundreds in our wake, but the end of it was that God's purpose was not served. We became objects of ridicule and scorn, as the people believed the damsel to be in alliance with us, or we with her, in her sort of mysticism. The blessed Saviour of whom we spoke was taken by the pagans as merely a new deity to be added to the already abundant supply.

So the end of it was that my patience began to be sorely tried. At last, when the damsel cried out her screeching mockery, I wheeled around and rebuked the evil spirit within her, saying: "I command you in the name of Jesus Christ to come out of her!"

She fell back against the wall of a building and threw her hands to her head and screamed. All those round about stood stunned, and watched as the damsel slowly lowered her hands.

131

Her face thus revealed was relieved of its contortion, and she was even pleasant to look upon. The horrible, disfiguring tension was gone from her body, and she stood as one possessed of inner calm. And straightaway she turned and walked peacefully through the crowd.

Then we went back to the theme of our message, but addressing now a crowd from whom there issued no mockery. Struck silent by the power of God shown through his servant, they listened and continued to attend our words for the greater part of an hour.

Hearts were being touched, and I was to the point of issuing the invitation to Christian discipleship when shouts rent the air. We turned to see at least a half dozen men pushing their way through the crowd.

"Seize the false teachers!" they cried. "They preach insurrection against the great god Caesar!"

And they continued to shout and to stir up the people with fear until hands were laid on us and we were dragged through the streets to the center of the marketplace. There, after a mock trial before those calling themselves the magistrates, we were beaten with staves until our blood ran in the streets and we fell into unconsciousness.

When we awoke, we had been cast into a filthy cell, populated by a dozen emaciated, heavily shackled, half-dead men, whose stench remains in my nostrils to this day. As the first light of consciousness began to dawn upon me I was being prepared for the stocks, and Silas, barely conscious, moaned in his pain. He was seated to my right, his bloodied ankles fast in the stocks. His head hung down on his chest dripping blood from a wound in his temple. I felt the wood clamp down on my own ankles and heard a curse from the man who had secured me. The heavy door clanged shut. We were in semi-darkness, though it was mid-day.

Soft groans and muted whispers echoed in the dank hollow as my first strained inquiry of my friend went unanswered. Hours passed before he was able to speak coherently, and then a miraculous thing happened.

We were not fed nor in any wise attended, but the healing hand of the Lord was laid upon us, and though the pains did not greatly abate, our minds were restored. We began to pray, and then to sing. Never had I been so powerfully constrained to sing. We joined our voices in a hymn of praise and the resonant chamber rang with our singing. For hours we sang, and shouted the praises of God to the other prisoners. After a time we attracted a gathering outside the window of our cell. When we knew the people were there, we began to speak the message of salvation.

About the hour of midnight, we had grown exceedingly tired, and the crowd outside had dispersed. We had prayed and had sat in silence for some minutes when there was a sudden, violent tremor and a loud rumble, like the sound and effect of a landslide.

Bits of mortar and rock pelted the floor around us, and the foundation of the building seemed to give way. The floor on which we sat sank to one side, and the cell door flew open as if jerked back violently by a mighty hand. The stocks cracked apart, and we heard elsewhere the clank of chains falling to the floor. Men spoke out, some in terror, others in reaction to sudden freedom, for all chains were loosed in the jail. My friend and I, amazed as the rest, stayed crouched to the floor, being loosed of our bonds, and did not move until the tremor had passed.

Now the jailer, having been rudely awakened by the commotion, ran from his station, and seeing all the cell doors open and supposing his prisoners to have fled, drew his sword to kill himself. But I saw him and called out to him to do himself no harm but to get a light and come in to see that no man had escaped, the others there being too weak from beatings and starvation to have fled in any case. This he did, and in awe and thanksgiving fell down prostrate before us. When we bade him arise, he motioned us outside, and out of the hearing of the others, asked "Sirs, what must I do to be saved?"

I said "Believe on the Lord Jesus Christ and you shall be saved." Then we spoke to him of the Lord. He was as a child, not bitter and cursing now as before, attending every word we spoke, humble, penitent, his eyes wide and reflecting the light of the lantern he had set on the table beside him.

133

"You must come to my house, sirs," he said, "and tell my wife and my children these things."

So we went with him and ate of the food his wife set before us. When they had washed our wounds we spoke again the good news of salvation and that night baptized the jailer and his wife and their three children. Afterward, not wanting to bring down the wrath of the magistrates on the jailer, we returned to our cell and there remained until the following day.

Shortly past dawn, representatives of the magistrates, who feared the people, seeing that the people attributed the manifestation to our God, came to the cell with orders for our release, but we did not move.

"You have beaten and condemned openly two citizens of Rome and have thrown them into this filthy prison," I said, "and now you seek to cast us out unknown to the wicked. You tell your masters to come here themselves and face us openly and see this awful place where men are thrown unjustly and left to rot."

The envoys left, returning shortly with their masters, a pompous group like many we had seen. One, short and fat and attired in a rich white robe tied with a purple sash, addressed himself to me. "Seeing that you are Romans, you are free to leave," he said in a deep voice which rumbled up from within the rolls of fat which his robe could scarce conceal. "But do not set foot again in this city, or you may not find us in so charitable a mood."

"For what crime were we imprisoned?" I asked. "Under Roman law is it not our right to know?"

"For the crime of sedition against Caesar."

"What sedition?" asked Silas.

"You spoke of allegiance to a dead Jew," said the fat one.

"You spoke of a King of kings," said another. "I was there and I heard."

"We spoke not of an earthly king," said Silas. "Jesus Christ said, 'Render unto Caesar that which is Caesar's and unto God that which is God's.' At no time have we preached sedition."

The fat one spoke again. "Caesar is both god and man, therefore all things are his. Now, get you out of the city, and do not return." He stepped back, and as he did so the haughty group opened a path among them.

I turned to the wretches on the floor and against the walls. "You men, who have heard the truth of Christ and seen the mighty hand of God, stand fast in the hope whereof we have spoken, and God will bless you. Do not cease to pray, and do not cower before these jackals." We walked through the midst of the magistrates and made our way out into the blinding light of day.

We had gone no more than three blocks toward the inn where we had rooms, when, through the early morning press of shopkeepers and workers we heard my name called out by the voice of a woman. We stopped and turned to see the damsel, now fresh and clean of her impurity, approaching from the row of buildings.

"Sirs," she said when she stood beside us, "I have been cast out by my masters, who stirred the mob to beat you, and I have nowhere to go."

I looked into her face and knew the sincerity of her words, and I took her hand.

"You may come with us," I said. The three of us went to Lydia's house, being greeted there joyously and with thanksgiving to the Lord.

The lovely Lydia had remained at home that morning, not knowing what had happened to us nor whether, indeed, we lived or were dead. Luke and Timothy were with her, and I recall the expression of Luke when I presented to him his patient, completely cured and full of the joy of the Lord. I believe he thought there had been a case of mistaken identity, for at first he could only shake his head. But when he knew it was the damsel, his joy was complete and he took her aside and plied her with those questions which are the special province of the physician.

We left that same afternoon, not in fear but in confidence that the Philippian church rested in good hands. Lydia had told us that many, knowing of her faith, had come to her and that times and places of regular worship were being arranged. For us, Thessalonica, Beroea and the region of Achaia lay ahead, untouched by the gospel, and the Lord had indicated to me that we must go on.

Luke and Helen stood by the gate, and Silas and Timothy were putting our things in readiness. Lydia stood in the doorway, and that is the picture I carry of her.

"When will I see you again?" she asked.

"I pray it will not be long," I said.

"You know you will always be welcome in this house," she said. "And Timothy and Silas."

"We have never felt more welcome at any place. We shall never forget your kindness."

She smiled and started to speak, but the words seemed to stop in her throat.

"May I write to you?" I asked.

"That is the only condition under which I will let you go," she said.

I turned while she was smiling and did not look back. Later, when I wrote, it was to the church at Philippi and not to her as I had promised. I pray her understanding of what I was, and am, and would have been . . .

We followed the wide Egnation Highway west to Thessalonica, twice being passed by fast stepping consignments of Roman troops outward bound. Arriving at that city we went straightway to a synagogue of the Jews and reasoned there three days. Some of them believed as well as some of the Greeks and a good number of women, toward whom we now found ourselves directing a greater portion of our ministry.

We encountered in this city one who believed in Christ, Jason, an honorable man who showed us much kindness, insisting even that we live in his house while we preached in Thessalonica. The house is notable in my memory, for the room in which I slept afforded a view of Mount Olympus, whose gods and goddesses I was soon to encounter in a most discouraging way.

Within a week of our arrival the legalist Jews had stirred up the people through a band of base men, accusing us of preaching sedition against Caesar. Finding ourselves set about by these lewd ones one night, we fled to the house of Jason and were thence spirited away by some of the brethren to Beroea.

But Jason and others were taken and dragged through the streets to the rulers of the city and accused of false crimes, among them "turning the city upside down with a false doctrine." Jason was released, but not until suffering humiliation before the citizens of his city.

In three days, Silas and Timothy and I were in a synagogue of Beroea, being, as I have said, received graciously by open-minded Jews. Many of them were saved, and we thanked God. We were also blessed in Beroea by receiving into the faith not only Greek men but also a goodly number of Greek women of honorable estate.

But when legalist Jews of Thessalonica heard of the works we were doing in Beroea, they came there also and stirred up the people so that I was asked by the brethren, for my own safety as well as the safety of others, to leave the city. The situation arose so suddenly and was so immediately critical that Silas and Timothy and I were forced to separate. I sent Timothy back to Thessalonica. Silas remained in Beroea. Both were to join me later in Athens.

Escorted by two of the brethren, I sailed south toward the ancient seat of pagan intellectualism, my thoughts steeped in gloom.

But as the hours passed, my spirits rose. We sailed calmly by historic Thermopylae. There the three hundred had stood bravely in the path of the barbarian horde. We sailed by the fabled isle of Salamis. There the valiant sons of Achaia had saved this culture from extinction. A victory for the Lord Jesus Christ here in this land would be a triumph of limitless proportions!

When we laid anchor at the port of Athens, my escorts left me. I was alone for the first time since my sojourn in Arabia.

But what can I say of Athens? It was all I had expected and more. Even five hundred years after that which we call its golden age it remained a scene of unparalleled splendor.

I walked through streets filled with gleaming marble sculptures stretching in geometric perfection beneath the regal Acropolis, crowned and splendid with its matchless Parthenon. I stood spellbound by the triumphs of the genius of man as displayed in the magnificent libraries and schools, the superbly planned marketplaces, the amphitheaters—like the theater of Dionysius which has a thousand marble seats. Never had I seen the human form so skilfully reproduced as in the masterpieces of statuary executed by the great Phidias. Everywhere abounded man's creative capacity.

But if this evidence of human intellect's triumphs impressed me, the abundant display of its failure struck me even more deeply. Here was intellectualism without God.

The city was completely pagan and morally bankrupt. Here, where Socrates had stimulated thought to unknown realms, men wallowed in the mire of godlessness. On one street I passed successively the temples of Minerva, Diana, Victory and Venus and encountered altars to Love, War, Fame, Pity, and Modesty. I learned that there were more than three thousand such places where men debase themselves before idols of their own construction. Here, where Plato had sought new truths and where Demosthenes had held forth in oratory, men and women without God clung to old lies and silent idols.

The optimism I had entertained was soon shattered, for the Greeks had deafened themselves to truth. They were so far from God that their minds were walled bastions of vanity.

I began to speak in the marketplace, called the Agora, and there encountered those called the Epicureans, who hold that pleasure is the end of man, and the Stoics, who worship nature-produced deity. They scoffed, and disputed with all manner of foolish ramblings. I was thereafter, in the Agora and elsewhere, ignored as a babbler. It would have been better had I been stoned.

When word of the strange one babbling in the marketplace had reached exalted ears, I was taken to that place called the Areopagus, or Mars' Hill, a semicircular rise of granite in the shadow of the Acropolis.

This is the seat of the high court which sits in judgment of speakers, to decide whether they shall be allowed to appear before public audiences. Had I sought it, I could not have found a more perfect forum for expounding the Gospel. Within easy view stood the gold and ivory statue of Athena which looks down like a jealous mother over the city. Given leave to speak, I prayed God for the best words to reach these scholars and officials.

The Lord laid it upon my mind to use as reference those idolatrous things I had seen and could see. I proceeded, sparing no feelings, releasing that emotion which had welled up within me since the moment I had looked upon the first pagan temple of the city.

Not knowing whether at any moment I might be set upon with vio lence, I accused the Athenians repeatedly of the basest of iniquitie in affronting the one true God and laid the blame for their declin at their pagan feet. I called to their attention an inscription I hac seen on one of their altars.

"As I passed by," I said, "and beheld your devotions, I foun an altar with the inscription: 'TO THE UNKNOWN GOD.' Whom therefore, you ignorantly worship, Him declare I unto you."

Using this as a point of departure, I launched a verbal assaul upon their constant seeking after complete truth but refusing to atten its revelation. Here in this 'unknown god' was represented som occurrence they could not comprehend or ascribe to any manufacturec deity. I progressed to the subject of creation, proceeding thence through the logical sequence of revealed truth, constantly referrin to philosophical quotations from their own respected thinkers and tc the most high God, Whom I held ever as the source of my ow life and philosophy of life. From God to the Son of God my dis course continued as a discourse of logic. If man had sinned anc God was just, then a mediation for sin was required, even as the offered mediatorial sacrifice. The god they called "unknown" I helc to have been revealed in the form of Jesus Christ, Whom they coulc accept and thus stand cleansed before their Creator. And as testi mony to the true deity of Christ, I offered the story of his ascensior from the grave.

When I had finished I was simply dismissed. No stones were cast. No rods were laid across my back. No mob dragged me before the authorities. As in the Agora, those gathered simply laughed or turned away and left. The judges said that they woulc hear me again at a later date, then they arose and departed, leaving me alone in the lengthening shadows.

So I stood until they all had gone, until the silence sealed my total defeat and the lips of Athena seemed to curve into a triumphan and diabolic smile. I descended Mars' Hill and lost myself in the throngs of the city.

The only light in the dismal Athens experience was the coming forth of a handful, notably and incredibly one Dionysius, a judge o

he court, and the woman, Damaris, who had heard me speak. She
brought her family, and they all were baptized.

Shortly thereafter, on a gray and gloomy morning, I departed
Athens for the city of Corinth. I spoke to no man along the way,
but walked enveloped in the shroud of depression which drove the
light from my spirit as the clouds obscured the light of the sun.
My thoughts returned to those things which have stabbed at my inner
being at maddening intervals through these years. Rachel was gone
forever, and I had not been able to find Ephraim to speak to him,
to beg his forgiveness. Stephen's head lay bloodied beneath the rocks,
and children and old men cried out in pain and hunger. Again and
again the thoughts and pictures returned, and the closer I drew to
the great center of commerce, where men who were not completely
involved in their financial enlargement were sunk in the depths of
pagan iniquity in the worship of Venus, the more seriously I considered turning back to Philippi. But God spoke to me and bade
me continue that his purposes might be served.

Thus reinforced, I entered Corinth and found the city to be
beautiful, and new in all respects. It had been totally rebuilt under
order of Julius Caesar after having been laid waste by war, and its
gleaming edifices rose resplendent in the sun. It is a planned city,
and, in the refinements of its design, incomparable on earth. But I
had not then nor have I now any optimistic thoughts concerning its
future without God.

I sought employment on the street of the tentmakers, and there
encountered a man named Aquila, a Jew of Italy, in Corinth by
order of the Caesar Claudius who had expelled all Jews from Rome.
This Aquila was a good man, and righteous, who gave me work to
do in his shop, and later, with his wife Priscilla, accepted the Lord
as Saviour. I think often of these saints and remember them in my
prayers.

Weekdays I toiled in the shop of Aquila, and each Sabbath spoke
in the synagogue of the Jews, encountering there as much hatred as
I had found in any place. My message failed to convert the legalists,
nor during the week could I dent the disgusting armor of sensuality
of the Greeks. I was surrounded by corruption and hated by the

141

Jews. My spirits sank to new depths, so that anger, for the first time since my conversion, gained control of my emotions. Returning hatred for hatred, I washed my hands of the Jews one sabbath, using language the like of which I have seldom employed. I left them and went to the Gentiles, being offered the use of the home of a good man named Justus to speak the truth of the Lord. But the groups who came to the house of Justus were small and this beginning, of what was to become a great church, was so seemingly insignificant that I went about with my head low and possessed of a deep melancholy. But in the midst of it the Lord came to me in a vision by night and said, "Be not afraid, but speak, and hold not thy peace; for I am with thee, and no man shall set on thee to hurt thee; for I have much people in this city." I took courage then and began to speak out for Christ with renewed vigor, on the streets and wherever there were those who would listen.

The Jews, thus aroused, fell on me in force one day in the market-place and dragged me before the Roman governor, Gallio. But the Lord fulfilled His word, and to the amazement of the Jews, Gallio dismissed them from the tribunal with a cynical rebuke. Whereupon, the very president of the synagogue, seeing the error of his way, accepted Christ, setting a magnificent example and causing conversions to multiply throughout the city. Nothing is outside the power of God.

Silas and Timothy had joined me, further lifting my spirits with news of continued success among the Christians of Macedonia, and bringing from the saints a gift of money. And now, when the tide had turned in the favor of the Lord, they continued with me in the city of Corinth for above a year, firmly planting the cross of Jesus Christ in the midst of the licentiousness of Achaia.

And now, that which was my second journey for Christ began to come to an end. God called us to cross the Aegean Sea to the city of Ephesus, in the west of the province of Asia, and we departed, taking with us Aquila and Priscilla. We remained only a short time, for I was anxious to return to Jerusalem and to Antioch, to be with the brethren there and to report the successes and failures of our mission. Aquila and his wife desired me to stay longer in Ephesus, but we had determined to be in Jerusalem at the time of the feast.

So Silas and Timothy and I departed by ship for Jerusalem, and went from there to Antioch to report to the church.

Our return was a triumphal one, and the news we brought was enthusiastically received. Timothy gloried in expounding his adventures and spent much time among the youth, while Silas and I recounted the Macedonian story to the elders. Nor did I fail to report my fiasco in Achaia.

But for all the positive news we brought, the reports we heard were disturbing and cast a shadow over our spirits. There were accounts of strife between the Jews and the Romans in Jerusalem. Open hostility toward Roman authority had broken out, and many deaths had resulted. But to us, the most disturbing reports were those concerning perverted teaching in the churches of Galatia. There, where I had thought Christ to be most firmly established, the legalist false teachers had infiltrated. Professing to be converted Christians, they had set out to overturn the faith of the believers, teaching that I was no real apostle and that I had no right to go about accepting uncircumcised Gentiles into any body of Jews. Pretending to be true church authority, these men were, with some success, warning the brethren in Galatia to turn from the ways I had taught them and to reestablish the ways of legal Judaism or be expelled from the church. This news frightened as well as infuriated me, for I could see crumbling all that had been so laboriously established. The damage that this renewed outbreak of false teaching could do to all Christianity was staggering to contemplate. My immediate thought was to make a swift journey to Galatia, but God laid it upon me instead to put into a letter all those things which reposed so heavily on my mind.

So I wrote an epistle to the Galatians into which I poured the burden of my soul, reminding them of the faith which had been placed in them and expressing my concern lest this faith had been placed in vain. I reminded them of the prophecy which Christ had fulfilled with his coming, and of the truth that before God there are neither Jew nor Greek, neither bond nor free, neither male nor female, but that all are one in Christ. I admonished the Galatians to open their eyes to see these infiltrators for what they were, and to recall that this thing had happened before, and had been settled in the case of Titus. My epistle was one of dismay that some of them could so easily be swayed from the truth, and I closed with a reference to the many wounds I had received in the service of Christ. No apostle has suffered for the Lord as I have suffered. Suffering is my badge of apostleship.

God spoke through the letter, for the subsequent news we received from Galatia told of increasing ejections of the infiltrators and of a general reestablishment of the faith. And God spoke to me. The letter can be a powerful force for Christ.

The beginning of my next journey came shortly after we received the good reports from Galatia. My immediate objective was a revisiting of the Galatian churches in Lystra, Derbe, Iconium, and the Pisidian Antioch for the purpose of reassuring the brethren of our love and constant support. This was accomplished, a high point being the reunion of Timothy, grown mature in the faith now, with his mother and his grandmother.

Silas did not accompany us on this journey, as it had been decided that he could be of greater service to the Lord in Jerusalem. But Timothy stood at my side as we returned through Asia.

Not since I had first set foot in Ephesus had the city been out of my mind, and immediately upon quitting Antioch-in-Pisidia we turned in that direction, arriving in the same month. This Ephesus was a city apart. For sheer beauty it rivaled Athens and Corinth, but surpassed both in wealth, being located near that place where the Maeander River empties into the Aegean. For unbridled sensuality it outstripped any place on earth that I have seen. The people, I found to be given wholly to pleasures of the flesh, having created numerous edifices for their vain satisfaction. A magnificent theater and a race track drew spectators from across the civilized world.

Superstition was rampant. The goddess Diana was worshiped in a temple whose proportions and appointments staggered the imagination. It was said that one hundred and twenty years were required for its construction, as it was built of solid marble and surrounded by twin rows of towering, fluted pillars. One entered the sanctuary from any direction by means of marble steps, and upon standing inside was confronted by a square of closely placed pillars of green jasper. Within the hollow recess thus formed there was a secret chamber housing an altar carved by the sculptor Praxiteles and a wooden figure of the goddess Diana shrouded by a purple curtain. The figure was hideous, and was never seen by the hordes of pilgrims who came from miles around bringing gifts to be hung upon the walls. Unscrupulous silversmiths sold shrines of the goddess to the pilgrims as mementoes, or peddled them in the outlying regions to those who could not worship the goddess in person.

So the scene on which we entered was, though on a grander scale, much the same as we had found elsewhere. The Gentiles were totally separated from any knowledge of the truth, and the legalist Jews were so blinded by their own self-righteousness and futile seeking after impossible goals that they hated the purveyors of the truth. Immediately upon reentering Ephesus I went to the synagogue, but, encountering the usual opposition, was thrust out.

God sent me then to a man named Tyrannus, a teacher who owned a school of some renown, and I made a business transaction with this Tyrannus whereby I was allowed the use of his facilities each day when his classes had been dismissed. For two years thereafter, each day after the hour of eleven, when public life in Ephesus was suspended to allow for private pursuits and for rest, the school was mine, and many were added to the faith.

Now there was in those days a man named Apollos, a Jew of Alexandria, who had arrived in Ephesus while Timothy and I were in the provinces. He had distinguished himself among those who knew him, chiefly Aquila and Priscilla, with the keenness of his intellect and the purity of his spirit. His testimony was for the Lord, but, though effective in its sincerity, was incomplete, for he had not been exposed to the whole truth. Somehow, he had come to a

146

knowledge of John the Baptist and his prophetic pronouncements, but he knew nothing of the Christ of those pronouncements, nor had he been previously associated with anyone who did. Nevertheless, this Apollos, with much fervor, went about speaking his message to all who would listen.

Therefore, when he became known to Aquila and Priscilla, they sought him out, listened to him preach, then invited him to their home. There, in hours of friendly discussion, they filled in the unknowns to this saint of the Lord, who received it all with eagerness. So wondrous a preacher did Apollos thus become that he was stationed in a position of the highest importance in the church at Corinth.

But God was no less with me. During the years of daily preaching in the school of Tyrannus many were saved and many were healed and the crowds daily increased. Our story was spread abroad throughout the region of western Asia, and Timothy was sent out as a missionary into Macedonia for a season.

So effective, indeed, was our ministry that those who sell the idols began to feel the pinch. Under the leadership of an evil man named Demetrius they were inflamed to the point of violence and formed one day into a mob intent on killing us or driving us from the city. For two hours they stood in the street, screaming: "Great is Diana of the Ephesians!" The authorities, being fearful for my safety, came and admonished me to stay clear of the mob. The town clerk was sent to reason with Demetrius and his followers, a mission eventually proving successful in the dispersion of the mob.

But to me, this was a twofold signal. It meant that the Gospel had reached a point of prime effectiveness in the region about Ephesus, and it also meant that, as the chief bone of contention between the pagans and the Church, my continued presence was not prudent. God's indication was that my time had come to leave. So I called a meeting of the church and spoke of my departure.

I did not like the thought of leaving them, for I loved them much. For the first time since my boyhood I cried. There were tears among the congregation, for we had been through much together. In a sense I was being driven from them, and my spirit carried the additional burden of bad news from Corinth, where legalists had again infiltrated. In a life of sad occasions, this final word to the Ephesians exists in my memory as singular. When I had said those things I had to say I went among the brethren, embracing them and imparting to each a special word of thanksgiving and of reassurance of the love and strength of the Lord Jesus Christ. Then we went as a body to the ship.

I knew the unspoken question among the Ephesians had been why I had chosen to sail north rather than west toward Corinth. I knew they had wondered why I had chosen to send Titus, who had joined us in Ephesus, instead of going myself to the trouble spot. I made no explanations.

I sailed toward Troas, having previously planned to meet Titus there and hear his report of the situation at Corinth. When the report had been given, I would set out for Philippi and see Lydia again. And after that, there might be Rome.

But Titus did not come. My stay in Troas was one marked by unrelenting depression in which nothing was accomplished for the Lord. Days passed and there was no word from Titus, so I took ship across the Aegean, landing at Neapolis and starting immediately from there toward Philippi.

The miles I would have once taken easily in stride came harder for man now grown old, and I suppose the difficulty was compounded by an old man's youthful eagerness to see one for whom he cared deeply. So what can I say of the state of my mind when they told me Lydia was in Rome? I had looked forward to seeing her. The disappointment hurt. I was very tired and very depressed, and I took a room at an inn and stayed there two days and two nights without food or sleep. It was thus Luke found me.

"You will come with me, to my house," he said.

"Do not trouble with me," I said.

"Trouble? It is no trouble. The trouble would be if you would not let me help. Why did you not come to me?"

I did not reply.

"You do not think much of your friends."

"I do not deserve friends. I have had friends and lost them."

"I cannot believe that."

"You cannot believe it because you do not know me. You do not really know me. I have caused more pain and sorrow than you can imagine."

He looked closely at me. "You are depressed . . ."

"For every success the world knows, I have had ten failures, and they have involved people who loved me and trusted me."

"Come, my friend."

"For all the trust God has placed in me, I am a failure."

Luke knelt beside me. "You have led countless thousands to Christ, and you are not pleased with it?"

"No. I am not pleased with my life."

He hesitated, choosing his words. "Paul, I think there is an elemental fact which has somehow escaped you. I hope you will not be offended in my saying it. A man does not have to be pleased, not totally pleased, either with himself or with his friends. He does not have to censure himself for his failures, because it is in failing that he gives meaning to success. Failure is as much a part of God's plan as is success, else wherein would man be man and God be God?

"You drive yourself to the limits of human endurance—and then sink into the depths of guilt when things do not go as you would have liked, or into the depths of disappointment when friends do not measure up to whatever it is you have decided a Christian should be. The happiest man is he who learns early that there is glory in imperfection. It makes the triumphs sweeter, and it saves a multitude of sorrows. Now come, my friend, and do me the honor of allowing me to repay you for all that you have done for me."

150

I took his hand and arose and we went out together to his house. Titus did come within the week. He had been delayed by conditions at Corinth. When he reached Troas he was advised by the brethren there of my departure to Philippi. The word he brought was so good that I thanked God for it as he spoke. The instigators of the turmoil at Corinth had been exposed for their true color, and order had been restored. So I sat down and wrote a letter to the brethren at Corinth, the second I had sent to them, and in it tried to reveal some of the things I had experienced as a disciple of Christ and to defend thereby my claim to apostleship. I sent the letter by Titus, and he had not been gone a day when Timothy arrived with greeting from the brethren at Ephesus, who had not ceased to pray for my well being since my leaving.

Within that month, Timothy and I were ourselves on the road to Corinth. Arriving there, we found all things going well for the Lord. I was received with love and advised extensively on the progress of the church. My stay of six months thereafter saw the completion of a letter to the Romans, whose city I had longed to visit from my youth. In this letter, dictated to a brother in the faith named Tertius, I wrote that all men, of whatever race, must be justified in the same manner: by faith in the Lord Jesus Christ. Having much time to spend on its composition, and perhaps entertaining the thought that Lydia's eyes might somehow see it, I poured my soul into each line. I tried to state, in as concise a form as possible, the whole truth of the Gospel as revealed to me.

As time came for me to depart Corinth, I laid plans for a sea voyage to Jerusalem and Antioch, but before the plans could be initiated word came that a band of legalist Jews lay in wait to kill me at the port of Cenchrea. So I determined to take Timothy and go back overland to Macedonia and Troas, and at Troas to book passage on another ship. It was also possible that Lydia had returned from Rome.

So the journey was undertaken, and it was to be one beset by some difficulties, for barely out of Corinth I cut my foot badly on a sharp stone and had to depend heavily on my son Timothy the remainder of the distance. Nor had Lydia returned from Rome.

151

Her house was closed tightly, and her women had received no word from her in weeks. This, of course, but compounded my misery, for my foot was by then badly infected. We found Luke and he attended to the wound, draining off the poison and wrapping the foot in yards of cloth spread thickly with a foul-smelling black substance made of herbs. The word of the physician was that I must stay off the foot for a while, but I told him I had no time to waste and that the Lord would heal my foot as he had healed a thousand other wounds. Shortly thereafter Luke asked if he might accompany us to Jerusalem and Antioch, and I do not know to this moment how much my physical condition had to do with his request. I do know that he has not left me since that day, and never has man had a more loyal companion nor the Lord a more devoted servant.

We sailed for Troas and dwelt there a week during which time a church was established for the Lord. During that week a certain incident occurred which I must include, for it further serves to illustrate the power of God. We were holding our final meeting in a hot and crowded building which had been donated to our use by a brother in the faith. I had spoken long, until the hour of midnight, when suddenly a young man fell from a perch he had taken high in the rafters. His body plummeted to the hard floor and he was killed instantly. All the assembled rushed forward and crowded about the youth but I bade them step back, and I leaned down over the boy and prayed. He straightway rose up and took bread and left that night with his parents. The brethren rejoiced greatly, and praised the Lord for his goodness and mercy.

On the following morning we departed for the city of Assos, from which we would take ship to Jerusalem. Throughout my journey I had collected offerings from the brethren to be turned over to the apostles and I was increasingly anxious to discharge this duty as well as to see and to speak to those men. But I must confess that I felt something less than complete enthusiasm about that which might await me in the city. My experiences in Jerusalem had always been troubled, and to return there now in my sixtieth year when the place abounded with civil strife engendered no optimism within me. Nor did the condition improve, for at every port at which we touched I was prevailed upon by the Christian brethren not to continue to Jerusalem.

At Miletus, the elders of the church at Ephesus met our ship and expressed deep concern lest I face much travail, but I impressed upon them my determination to continue, and to face death, if that need be, for the cause of Christ. I told them that my work in Asia was finished and that they would see my face no more, for it was the will of God. These were sad times for me because I loved these people, and because there is no earthly pain which will compare with that experienced at the last sight of a loved one.

From Miletus we sailed south and east, touching the points of Cnidus, Rhodes, Patara, and Myra, and in each city being warned of them who are blessed with the gift of prophecy that much sorrow and trouble lay ahead. I will not imply that I was not afraid. Each new mile increased the fear, but I had a duty to discharge and it was too late in my life for me to think of running from danger. I would face whatever was in store, if not fearlessly, at least in assurance that I had kept the faith.

O ur voyage of many days ended at the port of Ptolemais, just north of Jerusalem. From there we walked the coastal road to Caesarea and stopped to rest at the home of Philip, a disciple who had distinguished himself mightily in the service of the Lord.

I spoke earlier of a mission of mercy on which Barnabas and I were called before the first missionary journey. This mission had to do with a great famine in Jerusalem and throughout Judea to whose victims we took relief from the Antioch church. This famine had been prophesied by one Agabus, a saint of the Lord, and it was in heeding his words that we were able to set aside for the needy.

While we rested in Caesarea we were visited by Agabus, now old, but still forceful in the service of the Lord. His words, too, warned of the fate which awaited me at the hands of the Jews. While Luke and Timothy and others stood by, Agabus removed the linen girdle from my waist and bent over and bound his own hands and feet and said: "Thus says the Holy Ghost. So shall the Jews at Jerusalem bind the man who owns this girdle."

I looked at him and said: "What do you mean by weeping and breaking my heart? For I am ready not to be bound only, but also to die at Jerusalem for the name of the Lord Jesus."

Agabus, seeing the determination of my heart, departed, having

154

accomplished his mission for the Lord. I was not mindless of the inspiration of his warning, but I suppose now that it must have seemed as though I was and that I was stubbornly and intentionally disregarding the word of the Lord.

Within the week we were in a changed Jerusalem, a Jerusalem whose streets were bathed in the blood of men caught up in a whirlwind of revolution. Daily both Roman and Jew fell before the blade, as those tensions which had been building through the years stood naked and exposed along the streets. Jewish terrorist bands known as the daggermen roamed the byways at night, killing both Romans and Jew, any whom they felt stood between them and freedom from the Roman yoke. In league with a political band known as the Zealots they had made a nightmare of life in the holy city.

But in the midst of it all, and paradoxically, the church was enjoying a season of comparative tranquility, as the Jews had directed their full attention against the Roman heel. My report and the money which had been delivered to my charge were directed to James, the brother of the Lord, who stood at the head of the church at that time. We were afforded every element of hospitality in recognition of our missionary services. In return, we were asked to enter into the spirit of tranquility which prevailed between Christian and Jewish authority at that time. In compliance with the request I shaved my head and took the Nazarite vow and went the following day to the Temple to worship alongside the Jews from over the world, this being the time of the feast of Pentecost.

Timothy was with me, and we had done little more than enter the portals when looking about, at the prodding of my son, I saw a group with vaguely familiar faces whose eyes were cast upon me beneath scowling brows. Somewhere, on some journey, Ephesus perhaps, I had fallen afoul of these men. They were legalists, and they meant me no good. For the first time in my life, and only then because of my promise to James, I sought an avenue of escape. The men were some distance away across a body of worshipers, so Timothy and I turned to retreat through the portal which lay directly behind us. But we found the way suddenly blocked.

"Seize him!" screamed one. "Seize the blasphemer!"

155

The congregation shocked rudely by the sudden outburst, stirred to near panic, for such were the times. Seeing the outstretched arm and the finger pointing at us, the crowd fell back in fear. Immediately, the three at the door fell on us and sent my son Timothy reeling to the floor. My robe was torn, and an elbow hit my eye and cheekbone, knocking me senseless for a moment. When I recovered we were being dragged from the place of worship by the crowd, possessed now of a hysteria. Outside the wall, in the court yard we were set upon with a flurry of fists and heels, and we put our hands and arms up about our heads and faces and rolled our bodies into balls, as we had learned to do. But hammerlike blows thudded into my back and kidneys, and I heard my son cry out in pain.

Then, as suddenly as it had all begun, the beating stopped and some of the mob ran away. Removing my hands from my face, I saw a consignment of Roman troups approaching, swords drawn, at a run. The officer, immediately assuming that I, as the chief target of the assault, had instigated some breach of the law, threw me in irons and inquired of the mob what I had done. Many of them had never laid eyes on me and had, merely in the temper of the times, given vent to their emotions at the prodding of the legalists, who had recognized me. So some cried one thing and some another, until the officer yelled for silence and took me away. With a look and a push I treated Timothy as an enemy, and he perceived my meaning and ran into the crowd to lose himself among them, and then go to James and the brethren.

Shackled in irons, I was dragged to the steps of the Castle Antonia with remnants of the mob, still screaming for my blood, at my heels. On the steps of the castle I begged the officer to let me address the mob, and he at first refused, saying: "Are you not the Egyptian who led an insurrection some years ago?"

And I said, "I am Paul, a Jew of Tarsus, and I beg you to let me speak to the people."

He looked at me and saw the sincerity of my pleading and gave me leave. So I began to speak, and as I spoke, the pain of my body left me. I told the story of my conversion and the message

156

' salvation through Jesus Christ and that I had been warned to stay
way from Jerusalem because of this very danger which had be-
llen me. But when I finished, the mob was even more enflamed
ıd they began tearing their clothes and, in their fury, throwing
ıst into the air and screaming for my blood. So the officer
:dered me brought inside the castle, where I would be tortured until
confessed to whatever crime I had committed.

But as I was being prepared for the torture, I said, "Is it lawful
·r you to torture a man who is a Roman uncondemned?"

Whereupon the officer's face became ashen and he made haste
om the torture chamber, returning with his superiors. I withdrew
om within my robe the packet of papers of Roman citizenship
hich I carried always, and after the chief captain had examined
em, he apologized profusely for my maltreatment and ordered that
be afforded the status of guest of the state until proper disposition
uld be made of me.

On the following day, the Jews, demanding their rights pertain-
g to the Temple and to another Jew, had me taken down before
e Sanhedrin. I stood in the very spot where the innocent Stephen
ıd stood and surveyed the rows of pious, cynical and self-important
ces of which mine had been one that quarter-century before.
nger boiled up inside of me. Or was it that guilt which the proud
ıll anger?

The high priest Ananias, consumed with hate for all that is
ghteous, his thin lips curled in a sneer, said: "You stand accused
' blasphemy. Where are your accusers?"

The mob screamed, and Ananias held up his hand, shouting for
lence. "Where are the two required by law?" he said.

The two arose and went through that despicable ceremony which
hated, calling forth elements of the law. My muscles tightened,
ıd before the second had finished spitting out the venom of his
isoned soul, I said in a loud voice: "Men and brethren, I have
ved in all good conscience before God until this day."

Whereupon the evil Ananias ordered a guard to smite me across
e mouth. With that stinging blow all restraint fell away and I
oked at the twisted face of the high priest and pointed a finger

at him and said: "You whited wall. You sit in judgment of me as in the law and then command me to be struck, which is contrary to the law."

Some of those assembled arose and screamed: "Do you revile the high priest of God?"

I said: "Would that he were not the high priest, for God has commanded us not to speak evil of the ruler of his people."

As a rabbi I had been trained in the letter of the law so that by definition I was and am a lawyer. So I seized upon an opportunity which suddenly became apparent to me. Half those assembled were Saducees, who believe there is no resurrection from the dead, nor angels nor spirit; and the others were Pharisees, who confess the opposite. I said: "Men and brethren, I am a Pharisee, the son of a Pharisee. Of the hope and resurrection of the dead I am called in question."

As the words left my mouth, a murmuring broke out among the council and the mob, and then open dissension, sorely displeasing Ananias. His shouts to order fell on deaf ears as the clamor rose to a high pitch concerning what disposition should be made of me.

Then some of the Pharisees arose and shouted: "We find no evil in this man. If a spirit or an angel have spoken to him, let us not fight against God!"

The Saducees arose and shouted with even greater force than before and shook their fists toward the Pharisees, and all the while old Ananias screamed for order.

Then the chief captain ran forward and commanded his men to take me in charge and to escort me from the chamber lest a full scale riot ensue and I be torn asunder. Thus was I taken from the midst and returned to the castle. The night following I was awakened from my sleep by a vision of the Lord, and he refreshed and restored my spirits, saying: "Be of good cheer, Paul, for as thou hast testified of me in Jerusalem, so must thou bear witness also at Rome."

I greeted the following day with renewed courage and with an optimism incongruous with my surroundings. Rome had always held a fascination for me both for its repute as the world's foremost city and for its offering therein an unlimited field of operation for Christ. So, knowing that my future in this respect had been sealed of the Lord, I set my thoughts away from any fear of the present and channeled them toward the hope of the future.

It was about midday when my door was opened and a lad of no more than twelve years was ushered inside by the guard. I was seated across the small room on the bare floor, and in the dim light I could not make out the boy's features.

"Uncle?" he said.

Uncertain of his words, I said, "Come closer, my son."

"Uncle, is it you?" he asked, approaching.

I looked closely at him. "It could not be . . ." I said.

"I am Saul," he said, "the son of your sister Ruth."

I looked at him, not able to believe what I knew must be true. Then tears came to my eyes, and I lifted up my arms and held them out to him. He came to me, and I held him tightly and could not restrain my tears. I do not know how long I held him, but I could not let him go. "My son, my son."

After a time I held him out from me and said, "Stand out where I can look at you. My, what a fine boy. How old are you?"

"Just thirteen, sir."

"My . . . and . . . and what of your mother?"

"She is well. She sends her love to you."

"Her love?"

"We are Christians, sir."

"Thank God. Thank God."

I held him closely again and then put him out where I could look at him. "You live in Jerusalem?"

"Yes, Uncle."

"And your father?"

"My father is a silversmith."

"A silversmith?"

"Yes."

"And you are his helper?"

"Yes."

"What a fine boy."

He smiled but his smile faded. "I come to warn you," he said.

"To warn me?"

"Yes. Your life is in danger."

"In what way?"

"Yesterday I was passing near the marketplace on an errand for my father when I heard men saying your name. I stopped and pretended to be looking at vegetables, and I heard them speak of forty men who have banded together with an oath to take your life. They are of the daggermen, and they have sworn neither to eat nor drink until they have killed you."

"You are certain of this, my son?"

"I am certain, and you must leave Jerusalem. They are everywhere."

"Will you repeat this to the chief captain, Saul?"

"I will."

His eyes did not leave mine, and I knew that he had spoken the truth. "Then go, my boy," I said. "And tell him exactly what you have told me."

He nodded and hesitated for a moment, then started to turn, and I pulled him close to me again. "Goodbye, Saul. Tell your mother . . . tell her that I love her very much . . . and that I will see her one day."

I let him go, and he went slowly to the door and knocked. When the guard opened to him he turned and looked at me and went out.

That night, under cover of darkness and surrounded by two hundred footmen, two hundred spearmen, and seventy men on horseback, I was transferred to Caesarea, the headquarters of the Roman garrison. As we went, my thoughts traveled the road of events which had brought me to that condition. What a commentary it was on the sinfulness of man that one ordained of God, whose only purpose in life was to bring the hope of eternal salvation, should have had to be protected by a small army from his own people! In every bit and piece of my life I could see the wondrous hand of God opposed time and again by the will of man, but always triumphant and always to a certain purpose. That was how I felt about what lay in store for me at Caesarea. There might be more tribulation, but I had God's word there would be Rome.

The procurator of Caesarea was a man named Felix, who, of all men I had known, I found most distasteful. He was a thin, pale, shifty-eyed, hollow-cheeked man whose position, I could only guess, had been given him in return for some service rendered Caesar. He seemed to enjoy toying with those fallen before his judgment. When, in five days, Jews came down from Jerusalem to bring charges against me, he sat by in his resplendent chair and listened with unconcealed amusement. I gave a complete defense based on the whole truth, and Felix knew it was the truth, but he did not release me; he waved us all away and announced that his decision would be forthcoming.

For two years he made no disposition of me. I remained in Caesarea, not so much a prisoner as an arrested guest of the state. Time and again the Jews came and attempted to have me released to their custody but each time were turned away by Felix, who declared that to his knowledge no crime had been committed. The fact of my Roman citizenship played greatly into the scheme of things, but the foremost consideration of the procurator was the possibility of a bribe. I knew this almost from the first, as did everyone else concerned. It was an open secret which the vacillating and patently incompetent Felix made no apparent attempt to conceal Frequently I was called into his presence, and though he always feigned interest in those things he had me say of Christ, I knew he was merely amusing himself. Luke was with me almost continuously being allowed to come and go unimpeded, for Felix desired to appear to be my benevolent protector rather than my jailer.

My room had a window which looked out across the wide expanse of the Mediterranean. I spent hours sitting beside it, gazing westward in contemplation and prayer concerning the brethren in Galatia and Achaia and Ephesus and in Macedonia and all those places I had walked for Christ. Lydia was never far from my thoughts. I wondered what the months and years had brought to her, if she were well and if she ever thought of me. Luke brought me news, but there was little of Philippi, as the distance was so great.

But the Lord had provided wisely in setting aside these two years. My body had been worn severely by the rigors of twenty years and more of hardship. The rest was sorely needed. While my body was refreshed, my mind also was strengthened. In the solitude, God spoke to me and gave me new insight into various areas of the truth, which I expounded after this arrest in letters to the Ephesians and the Colossians.

In time, the Jews, whose powers I have never underestimated succeeded in having Felix removed from his position. They realized that he had no intention of releasing me without a bribe, and they had no intention of offering a bribe. So Felix was dismissed under pressure and replaced by Porcius Festus, a man of as few moral compunctions as his predecessor, but of greater intelligence. Taking note of what the Jews had been able to accomplish with Felix, he began to seek ways of affecting my release to them. He went to Jerusalem and conferred with the leaders, and, after deliberation, agreed to allow their lawyers to come to Caesarea to prosecute my case.

This subsequent trial was no less a mockery than any of those

162

others I had experienced, the difference being that in this one I was formally charged with preaching insurrection against Caesar in Jerusalem by presenting Jesus Christ as King of kings. At this charge, Festus began to feel the pinch and asked me if I would be willing to go to Jerusalem to stand trial. He knew, as did Luke, who expressed immediate opposition, that I could never hope to escape the blades of the daggermen once outside the protection of his troops. But he feared for his own position should he attempt, like Felix, to frustrate the Jews. His mind was decided already, the question being put to me merely as a formality.

I resorted to the only recourse left to me, one having been decided upon by Luke and myself some days previously. I turned to Festus and said: "I stand at Caesar's judgment seat, where I ought to be judged. To the Jews I have done no wrong, as you well know. For if I be an offender, or have committed anything worthy of death, I do not refuse to die, but if there be none of these things of which the Jews accuse me, no man may deliver me unto them. I appeal unto Caesar!"

The procurator registered surprise, and a murmur went through the assembly of Jews. But Festus knew he could do nothing now but grant my appeal, for it was the law of Rome. After conferring with the council he closed the proceedings with the official order that I be transferred forthwith to the courts of Caesar Claudius.

Any hope I had entertained for a speedy trial vanished as days of waiting became weeks. Festus could not order that a ship be sent with one prisoner, but of necessity must arrange passage for all those within his jurisdiction under appeal to Caesar. Luke never left my side during these days, and I spent much time in prayer and preparation for facing the emperor.

Before the passage of the second month, King Agrippa of the Jews came from Galilee to pay his respects to Festus as the new procurator, and in short order my presence was commanded before their exalted personages.

This Agrippa was a large portly man with a long curly black beard. He wore purple and had about his neck a heavy chain supporting a gold medalion whose center was a ruby of great price. His sister was handsome but severe, dark of hair and eyes but very fair.

After only the most negligible preliminaries, the king leaned forward and regarded me inquisitively. "You are permitted to speak for yourself," he said.

I bowed and said that I would do so with great pleasure, encompassing all those things of which I stood accused. Then I felt the presence of God as if it were a pervading warmth. The words came forth as the waters of a fountain. I appealed to Agrippa as a Jew, with knowledge of the prophets, refuting with logic all the false charges originated of the legalists. I recounted my conversion experience on the Damascus road and declared my unflinching faith in the resurrected Lord. As I spoke of the Saviour and of his godliness, of how he had descended from heaven, been born as a man, had lived among men, performed miraculous works, been crucified, then had arisen from the tomb, Festus leaned forward in his chair and began shaking his head. "Paul," he said, "you are beside yourself. Much learning has made you mad."

But I said, "I am not mad, most noble Festus, but speak the words of truth and soberness." I turned to Agrippa. "The king knows these things. None of this of which I speak was done in a corner." I pointed toward the king. "King Agrippa, do you believe the prophets? I know that you believe they spoke of Christ."

The king's gaze did not leave me. He said, "Almost you persuade me to become a Christian."

Then I said: "I would to God not only you, but also all they who hear me this day, were both almost and altogether of such persuasion as I am."

The king continued looking at me, his mind turning over all those things of which I had spoken. I prayed that he might fall on his knees before God and accept Christ. It would have been the greatest triumph for the Lord of my life. But it was not to be. The king slowly arose, then all those assembled. He walked out of the room.

By the time arrangements had been completed for transporting the full consignment of those whose cases were under appeal, it was late in the year and the time when it is unsafe to be on the sea. But this was of little concern to the procurator, who was glad to be seeing the last of us, particularly myself. The men who were to sail with me were two hundred and seventy-six in number and withal, beside the Roman guards, a crude and rough mixture of thieves, murderers, and alleged perpetrators of every crime imaginable. My status was still one of distinction, though relative, and I was allowed the company of Luke and the Christian brother Aristarchus. Our first in command was a Roman officer of the Imperial Regiment named Julius.

Our first stop, after departing Caesarea on a cold and windy day, was the ancient port of Sidon. Julius allowed my two companions and myself to go ashore and visit there the Christians, who refreshed us with good food and drink. But when the time had come for our departure the weather had worsened, and as we set out northward the waves rose to great heights and tossed our ship about like a log in a rapid. Many of the men became ill from the tossing of the vessel and others became severely frightened lest we be overcome by the waves and drowned, though Julius ordered the ship at all times kept in sight of land, following the southern coast of Asia. We passed by Myra and Patara, through the straits of the island of Rhodes, by Cnidus, thence south and west toward the island of Crete. After many days and nights of battling the elements we reached the port of Fair Havens on the south of Crete and put in for repairs and supplies. Some of our men were sick, but none had been lost.

The ship being safely anchored, Luke and I sought out Julius and prevailed upon him to lay in for the winter, as I had been warned in a dream that to continue was to court disaster. But he would have none of it, fearing lest even one of his prisoners escape and he be held accountable before Caesar. He declared also that the port was not fit to winter in, and that we, therefore, must sail immediately.

Not a whole day out of Fair Havens we were struck by a wind of such fury that we could not steer. Finally, we gave up and let the icy blast direct us as it would, not knowing whence we might be taken. In time we were set in on a certain small island which is called Clauda, and there we stayed briefly, making repairs to the ship. When the captain determined that we were seaworthy, we set out again. An hour out of Clauda we found ourselves again beneath black heavens and at the mercy of a mighty turbulence. This time we lightened the ship, throwing overboard the tackling. But the wind and waves did not abate. So powerful was the onslaught that all aboard except the three of us fell into panic, some dropping to their knees in frantic prayer and others running amuck across the deck. Luke had lashed himself to the mast, and I bade him take a strong grip on my arm while I stood on the small platform by the mast and called out to the men, for the angel of God had admonished me to this purpose.

"Listen to me!" I shouted. "Listen to me!" Again and again I called out until I had the attention of those nearby. "Men, listen! Do not despair, for God has spoken to me! There shall be no loss of life! No loss of life! We shall arrive safely at Rome! Do not despair!"

Whereupon, those who saw my face took courage and restrained their fellows. I spoke again that the Lord had said we should be cast upon a certain island.

Now on the fourteenth night, as we were driven up and down in Adria, the watch called out that we were drawing near some island. They sounded the depths and found the water twenty fathoms deep, and, when we had gone farther, found it fifteen fathoms. Then, fearing again for their lives lest we be dashed upon the rocks, the watch cast out four anchors off the stern and hoped for daylight, the night being totally black. Soon, panic again overtook the crew and they began to abandon ship, lowering a lifeboat.

Seeing what was happening and knowing that it was against the will of God, I rushed forward to Julius and shouted to him, "Except these abide in the ship, you cannot be saved!"

The crew, hearing my words, cut the ropes and let the lifeboat drop into the sea.

When the first rays of sunlight began to appear through the clouds on the following morning, I went forward and addressed the men and told them to take food, which they did gladly, not having eaten for days. I reminded them again as they ate that not one hair of their heads would be harmed. They all rejoiced and took cheer in the words of God.

When we had eaten, we again lightened the ship and cast the wheat, which was part of our cargo, into the sea. As the day broke full we surveyed the island. No one knew what land it was, but it was so welcome a sight that we made preparations to set into a cove, the mouth of a river, which we could see through the early morning haze. The rudder bands were loosened and the sail was raised and we made for shore.

Suddenly the ship went aground with a thundering sound and a violent jar which threw us to the deck. Immediately the stern was torn off by the force of the waves, for the bow was stuck fast, and the men at the back were separated from us. Some of the soldiers shouted that the prisoners must be killed lest they escape now that land lay before us and the ship was destroyed, and they took up their spears. But Julius restrained them, and commanded that all who could swim should dive into the sea and make for the island. Those who could not swim found boards and pieces of the ship and floated to the land. No man was lost.

We had not been long on the land when natives came and greeted us. The place, we learned, was the island of Melita, which lies a short distance south of the larger island of Sicilia.

The wind being severely cold and the men wet from the swim to shore, we began gathering sticks for a fire. Soon there was a good blaze, and I came and threw a last bundle of twigs upon it and felt, as I did, a pricking in my hand which I thought to be from a thorn. One of the natives cried out and pointed, and I looked down and saw a poisonous serpent wrapped around my hand and wrist. I immediately shook off the beast into the fire and went on about my business. At this the natives marveled, not knowing of the promise of God that I should reach Rome unharmed. When there came no swelling or ill effect, they began to regard me with some awe, as a god, but I rejected such treatment by ignoring it.

Within the day we were sent greetings by the governor of Melita, whose name was Publius. At his invitation we came and stayed in his house for three days. He was a good man and a charitable one. He saw to the fair disposition of the prisoners and to the supplying of all needs.

On the second day of our stay with the honorable man, Julius came to me and advised that the father of Publius lay sick of a fever in another part of the lodgings. So I went to him and prayed for his recovery, and he rose up forthwith and took food. Thereafter, many of the sick of the island came to me and went away healed. Our fame was spread abroad, so that we were honored of the people of Melita and supplied with all our wants for the space of three months.

When the last icy winds of winter had passed and the sea was calm again, Julius arranged passage for his troops and for the crew and prisoners on a ship of Alexandria which had spent the winter docked on an isle nearby. So bidding farewell to Publius and to hundreds of those of Melita who had come to see us off, we set out toward Syracuse, where we delayed for three days, taking on cargo, then sailed to Rhegium, through the straits of Sicilia, then up to the port of Puteoli, just south of Rome.

And now, as those things I desired to say draw near to the present and as I know not what each new day may bring I pray God grant me a blessing of time. Timothy should be here soon with the cloak I left at Troas and with those other things I requested, and I shall be most happy to see him. Luke has not left my side, having ministered to my needs continually.

The physician was with me as we approached Rome down the great Appian Way and heard, above the clank of the marching Romans, the bustle of this foremost city of the world. I thought, as the signs of Roman glory and grandeur began to appear more abundantly, how strange it was that I, who had wanted to capture the city for Christ, was proceeding toward it bound in chains and bent and broken of body and spirit.

I am not so strong in the faith as the world thinks, being given at times to fits of melancholy, and such was the state of my mind that day. I must have been a pitiful sight for the natives to behold, trudging along on that highway by which their conquering legions came back in glory, an old, gray-haired creature sometimes leaning for support on the tall man beside him.

But as Christ has in all times in my life when I have been most in need, the Lord lifted my spirits in his miraculous fashion. At a small place outside Rome called the market of Appius, a band of Christians met our procession, and the noble Julius ordered a halt and allowed us to go to them. They bolstered us with the joy only a Christian can bring to his fellowman. When we departed the market they joined in behind and marched with us.

Only a short way thereafter, at a place called Three Taverns, we were joined by yet another faithful band who, mingling with their brethren, fell in with them in the march and so accompanied us through the gates of Rome.

At the place of our incarceration, the good Julius went before his superiors and made such an eloquent plea for the man he credited with saving his mission that I was afforded all the comforts of a guarded guest of the empire. There was no cell for me, but an apartment with bedding and writing facilities, and food carefully prepared and courteously served. Luke was permitted to stay with me, and it was in this place that he began setting down in final form those things he is recording of the actions of the apostles of Christ.

Within three days of our arrival, I had called the Jewish leaders of Rome to my apartment and had told them of the error of their legalistic Judaism and of the falsity of the charges the Jews of Jerusalem had brought against me. But they pled ignorance of my case, saying they had received no word in that respect from Jerusalem. After certain days of listening with interest about the new sect called Christians which abounded in their city, they rejected the truth. When I quoted from Isaiah about the hardness of their hearts and the deafness of their ears, they departed, disagreeing among themselves.

So, as the days passed and my case was repeatedly postponed, I turned my quarters into the seat of Christianity at Rome, converting one room into a meeting place, and set my eyes toward the Gentiles.

The first whose hearts I endeavored to capture for Christ were the guards assigned to me day and night. With each changing shift I was presented the opportunity of witnessing for the Lord, and I found most of these fine young men attentive and eager to hear more of him whom I glorified. Seldom did my words fall on deaf ears, either of the guards or of the citizens of Rome who were allowed to visit and to take part in the regular prayer meetings. Both Jew and Gentile came, and many were received into the body of Jesus Christ.

A big Negro slave named Onesimus came to me, a runaway from his master, Philemon, and disillusioned by the world which he felt had treated him mercilessly. We talked of Jesus Christ and of the freedom he brings to the human spirit, and of the love which he is and with which he invests the hearts of them who call upon his name. I saw Onesimus change and take on the spirit of Christ, a new creature with forgiveness in his heart. I sent him back to Philemon and have no doubt that they are now brothers in Christ Jesus, for Philemon is a Christian. I sent a letter to Philemon and one to all the Colossians by the faithful Tychicus, who has shown me much kindness here in Rome.

Others who came during these two years of witness for Christ were Aristarchus and Timothy and my beloved John Mark, to whom I showed especial love and tenderness. No ill feeling remained in my heart or in his, and I bade him greet the great servant of Christ, Barnabas, whom I love deeply and who even now labors mightily for the Lord. By these men and by Tychicus and Epaphras I dispatched letters to the churches and was kept informed of the activities of the brethren.

The brother in Christ, Epaphroditus, came with things from Philippi to be used for my bodily needs, and I thought of Lydia and of all the Philippians. I dispatched a letter which I trust is in her hands. God's blessings upon the church at Philippi, and upon the gracious woman.

A letter was also dispatched to the saints at Ephesus, and on its completion I prostrated myself before God and thanked him for his mercy in allowing me this time. This time of bondage, toward which I had looked on the Appian Way with such heaviness of heart, had turned out to be one of the blessed periods of my life.

But if these were days of fulfilment for me, they were also the beginning of a period of unexampled horror for the children of God. The emperor, Claudius, under whose authority I had been dealt with so charitably, died and was succeeded by the monster called

Nero. It is said that this Nero has murdered both his mother and his half brother, has set his wife aside to marry an evil woman named Poppaea, and is responsible for the deaths of hundreds of Christians through unspeakable acts of madness.

It is an open secret that it was he who set fire to this great city, then sat by and watched most of it leveled to ashes. Luke and I stood at the window of my apartment that night and observed in horror as the flames licked skyward and as thousands jammed the streets and trampled one another underfoot. I hear yet the screams of panic and see the faces of those who scrambled for their lives beneath my window. I can only imagine the things for which this madman will be called upon to answer before the judgment throne of God.

This vermin-infested cell I now inhabit has been my dwelling place since the depraved man began his reign of terror on the followers of Christ. He is casting the blame for his arson on Christians and using that act as excuse to satisfy his satanic lusts. This cell is near the arena and I hear daily the tormented shrieks of men and women and children being torn apart by ravenous beasts to the delight of crowds of Romans gone mad while Nero, the man who calls himself a god, sits upon the throne. Surely God's judgment cannot be long in coming! Nero uses these maniacal diversions to occupy the minds of his subjects and to divert them from the ruin he is bringing upon the empire.

My cell has been the scene of much travail as Christians have lately been herded in and out like cattle being readied for the slaughter. There are so many that the prisons will not contain them. But there have been, even in this tribulation, many signs of the mercy of God. I have seen courage which puts me to shame, and I have seen acts of selflessness bespeaking the presence in spirit of the Lord Jesus himself. These Christians are invincible. They pray for their tormentors as they are beaten, and they sing as the lions are loosed before them. Praise God!

One night soon after the first part of my trial I was awakened by the captain of the guard, who knelt beside me holding a lantern. The cell was crowded with men, women and children, and the captain had sought me out from the midst of them. He bade me be silent, and motioned that I should follow him, which I did.

Outside the heavy door there stood a caped figure shrouded in the shadows, and when he motioned for the captain to leave us I could see that he wore the rich trappings of an official personage. When the captain had locked the cell door and left, the mysterious one threw back his hood and revealed a face I did not know, it still being half darkened in the shadows.

"Do you not know me, Paul?" he inquired.

I did not reply, thinking it to be some trick of the madman's.

"Do you not know the face of a Roman to whom you brought the good news of Jesus Christ?"

"There is something familiar, but I do not know . . ."

"Sergius Paulus, proconsul of Cyprus."

"My friend!"

I took his hand.

"God bless you, Paul."

"But what . . ."

173

"I am here at Rome now, a deputy to the Caesar. Does that surprise you? Do not answer. Let me say only that I serve the Lord still, in ways I could not serve him otherwise."

"Of course."

He glanced about. "Now, I must speak quickly and be gone. It was only at great risk that I came."

"Speak of what, my friend?"

"Of your escape. I have a way to get you out of here and out of Rome. You are of no value to the Lord and to his people in the shadow of the headsman's axe. Your doom is sealed. That first trial was no more than a mockery. Nero wants your life, and he will have it if we do not act in haste."

I could not speak.

"Your next trial is scheduled for one week from today, so we must act within that time. Now the captain of the guard here is a Christian. His name is Marcellus, and he is in charge of the night watch. Have you a cloak with a hood?"

"I have sent for a cloak and expect a young man with it at any time."

"If he does not come within two days I will get one to you. At all accounts, the plan is this. Four nights hence at the hour of eleven two visitors will come to call on Paul. One will wear a cloak with a hood and will remain silent. What color is your cloak?"

"Brown."

"He will wear a white cloak. The other will speak. They will be met at that door." He pointed to the end of the corridor. "They will be met by a guard and the captain Marcellus. They will be allowed to enter, and the guard will be dismissed on some pretext. It will be a thing of minor importance so as not to arouse suspicion.

"That which follows will have to be done in haste. The cell door will be opened, and you will step out and throw on the hooded cloak. I will have been that man and I will step back outside the corridor and be knocking when the guard returns. The captain will bid the guard open to me, and I will enter and inquire what the two men are doing at the cell door.

"At this, the captain will explain that they have come to see Paul,

174

and I will become very angry, redressing the captain for his stupidity in allowing visitors to enter at so late an hour to see a prisoner of such importance as Paul. The captain will begin to offer an excuse which I will refuse, demanding the visitors be sent out at once. This will be done straightaway, as the captain offers profuse apology which I reject, threatening disciplinary action.

"Then I will go into the cell, on pretense of checking on you, and, in the light of the lantern carried by the guard, I will pretend to inspect a dummy you will have made of your cloak. Satisfied, I will leave. Your escape will be thus assured. You can be miles away by the time the ruse is discovered. By then, I shall also be some distance away, and gladly."

"I understand, but ..."

"Shh, the guard returns. Now remember, four nights, the hour of eleven."

I did not reply as he put the hood back over his head.

"Let him back into the cell," he said, as the guard drew near. Sergius then disappeared in the darkness of the corridor.

Now I did not sleep that night, but prayed and turned the matter over continuously. It was true that I could be of no further service to the Lord if my fate were to be as described by the Roman. Luke, when he had been allowed to visit me, had spoken again and again of the need of a strong hand in Thessalonica. The legalists were again active in that region and had subverted many. I thought of the Thessalonians, and of Lydia nearby. Then there was my sister, whom I had not seen since her childhood, and that fine boy, her son. Had not the Lord himself sent me to Sergius and now Sergius to me? A coincidence? Surely not. Sergius had been saved to a purpose even outside the redemption of his soul. God had seen, in his infinite wisdom, what course the days were to take and had sent this man as my release for the purpose of returning to his church in this hour of its greatest need. A father is not asked to abandon his children at the time of their gravest peril.

So by sunrise my mind was decided. I would seize the opportunity God had afforded and return to a greater challenge than any I had ever known. I had good years left to me. That day and the day following I ministered to the condemned saints with renewed vigor, reinforcing their faith in the very face of death. They came to me in tears and left radiant in the hope of soon being in the presence of him for whom they would be called upon to die.

On the afternoon of the second day, Timothy came and brought me my cloak and the writing materials I had asked for. I whispered to him of the plan and his face brightened with that glow I had first seen and loved those years before. We arranged a meeting place, and he assured me he would have passage for two booked on a ship destined for Macedonia.

Even as we spoke, and as he waved goodbye to me at the cell door I knew I would never see my son again. I could not, of course, run away while my children were being devoured by beasts. I have written another letter to him, and he will know in reading it why a man must do what he must do.

There is a child here, one who is very young and very frightened. She is a beautiful girl with dark hair and eyes and skin as soft as the skin of a babe. The world had only begun to open for her when she was snatched away and cast into this place. She has seen her parents die a horrible death, and she is deeply grieved and much afraid. She is a Christian, but one who is not yet ready to die for Christ.

She will wear the hooded cloak two nights from now. She will accompany Timothy in my stead and will, I have no doubt, be accepted as a daughter in the home of Lydia. May God bless them all and keep them.

My last prayer shall be that much joy shall be theirs in the service of Jesus Christ, to whom be glory and honor, dominion and power both now and forever more, amen.